CRAZY
FOR CODY

An Unauthorized Biography by PJ Gach

PRICE STERN SLOAN

To Maxime Laboy—my pen-sister—thank you with all my heart; Joy & Rod; Michael B; Jax W; Jason S; Laura M; Elisa B; April C; The Bad Movie Club-Ben LeH, Matt P, Matt R, Jim D, Mo W, Isaac, Geraldine, Ryan—thanks!

And Mom, you were right!

PRICE STERN SLOAN
Published by the Penguin Group
Penguin Group (USA) Inc., 375 Hudson Street, New York, New York 10014, USA
Penguin Group (Canada), 90 Eglinton Avenue East, Suite 700,
Toronto, Ontario M4P 2Y3, Canada
(a division of Pearson Penguin Canada Inc.)
Penguin Books Ltd., 80 Strand, London WC2R 0RL, England
Penguin Group Ireland, 25 St. Stephen's Green, Dublin 2, Ireland
(a division of Penguin Books Ltd.)
Penguin Group (Australia), 250 Camberwell Road, Camberwell, Victoria 3124, Australia
(a division of Pearson Australia Group Pty. Ltd.)
Penguin Books India Pvt. Ltd., 11 Community Centre, Panchsheel Park,
New Delhi—110 017, India
Penguin Group (NZ), 67 Apollo Drive, Rosedale, North Shore 0632, New Zealand
(a division of Pearson New Zealand Ltd.)
Penguin Books (South Africa) (Pty.) Ltd., 24 Sturdee Avenue,
Rosebank, Johannesburg 2196, South Africa

Penguin Books Ltd., Registered Offices: 80 Strand, London WC2R 0RL, England

Photo credits: Cover: Gregg DeGuire/WireImage; Insert Photos: first page courtesy of Jason Merritt/FilmMagic; second page courtesey of John Sciulli/WireImage for John Varvatos; Jon Kopaloff/FilmMagic; third page courtesy of Gregg DeGuire/WireImage; Jemal Countess/WireImage; fourth page courtesy of Thos Robinson/Getty Images; John Shearer/WireImage

Library of Congress Control Number: 2009006966

ISBN 978-0-8431-8961-2   10 9 8 7 6 5 4 3 2 1

Contents

Dance Crazy

Monday, September 22, 2008, was a very special night in Cody Linley's life. That evening, the eighteen-year-old, green-eyed, shaggy-haired, blond star of Disney's *Hannah Montana* was going to make his dancing debut as the then-youngest competitor on the seventh season of ABC's *Dancing with the Stars*. Every day for a month, he and his *DWTS* partner, two-time *DWTS* champion and country music singer Julianne Hough, had practiced and perfected their moves.

Cody went through all the dance moves in his head again and again, making sure he knew his stuff. Then he decided to reach out to his fans before his big performance. Cody went online, logged in to his personal blog, and wrote, "Season 7 of *DWTS* starts TONIGHT sept. 22, and to kick it off I'm doing the cha cha with julianne hough. I'm super excited and I've been in dance rehearsals every day for the past month! Be sure to check it out live on abc at 5:00 p.m. (pacific time). Julianne and I are working really hard and if u vote, u can keep me on the show! So don't forget to vote!!! Please :). Call my new # and leave me a message 469-619-1240, and I'll be keeping you updated on everything I'm doing. Thanks y'all!!!"

The rest of the day went by in a blur, and soon it was time to head to the studio. Cody went into hair and makeup, and then spent a few minutes stretching and warming up so he'd be ready when it was his turn to dance. Before Cody knew it, it was time for the show to begin. Studio 46 at CBS Television City in Los Angeles was packed with *DWTS* fans. The on-air light flashed, the theme song came on, and host Tom Bergeron said, "This is the biggest *Dancing with the Stars* ever!" while the audience cheered and clapped.

There was no turning back!

Cody and his partner Julianne were ready to take the stage. Cody's hair was slicked back and he wore a black shirt under a black suit jacket. His pants had a thin, red stripe running down the legs and he had a red handkerchief square peeking out of his suit's breast pocket. Julianne wore a short, white, one-shoulder, sparkly dress with fringe trim and a red ribbon tied around one wrist.

When host Tom Bergeron announced, "First up, at eighteen, he's our youngest ever competitor and he's paired up with our youngest dancer, a two-time champion. It's *Hannah Montana*'s star Cody Linley and his partner Julianne Hough!" the couple made their way to the spotlight at the center of floor.

A version of "Tilt Ya Head Back" came on and they began to dance the cha-cha. As Cody and Julianne danced, the front of Cody's jacket moved away from his body and you could see that the lining was bright red! Their moves were crisp and well rehearsed. They were on fire. And it was clear that Cody and Julianne had serious chemistry!

When the song ended, the audience screamed and applauded. As the couple stood breathlessly in front of the judges, chief judge Len Goodman said, "You came out full of confidence. It was high-energy dancing . . . great job." Bruno Tonioli said, " . . . Channel the energy . . . keep it clean." And the best comment of the night came from judge Carrie Ann Inaba. She told them, and America, "What I see in you is incredible potential. I hope to see you tomorrow. I'm looking forward to it."

The duo received 18 of a possible 30 points for the cha-cha, which meant that they'd be coming back the following night. It was a very big night for Cody, but it was just one of many steps in a journey that started when Cody made his acting debut in 1998 at the age of eight in the made-for-television film *Still Holding On: The Legend of Cadillac Jack*. By the time Cody stepped through the backstage doors of Studio 46 earlier in the evening, he had already starred in eleven movies and appeared in three TV shows, including *Hannah Montana*. By the age of eighteen, Cody Linley was already a superstar!

chapter one

Meet Cody M. Linley

Cody Martin Linley was born on November 20, 1989, in Lewisville, Texas. His mom Cathy Linley, an acting teacher, and his father Lee Linley, the owner of a hair salon, eagerly welcomed their happy, green-eyed, baby boy into the world. Cody's big brother Chad was a very friendly seven-year-old, and must have really looked forward to having a younger brother to boss around!

When Cody was only one year old, his parents got divorced. Luckily, both parents stayed in Lewisville, so the brothers were able to spend time with their dad even though they lived with their mom. Cody's dad lived in a house only ten minutes away. When they were a little older, Cody and Chad could easily ride their bikes from one house to the other. Lewisville is a big town just north of Dallas, Texas. Lewisville was the perfect place for a little boy like Cody to grow up: It had woods, fields, parks, and Lewisville Lake, a great spot for fishing. Cody was a very active boy who loved playing outside. "My favorite time of day is sunset. I like nature and spending time outside looking at the stars," Cody explained to *BOP* magazine. As a kid, Cody was lucky to have an older brother like Chad. It was like having a built-in best friend, although Cody also had plenty of friends in the neighborhood and at school.

Growing up, Cody became really close with his mom, too. He learned a lot from her, and thought of her as his mom *and* his best friend. "Since I spent most of the time living with mom, she and I grew close," Cody told *M* magazine. A few years after the divorce, Cody's mom got remarried to a man named Brian Sullivan, a technical sales representative for PPG Industries. Cody's dad got remarried, too. Cody told

M magazine that when his parents got remarried, "At first, I was like, 'I don't know about this.' But I've actually loved growing up with two sets of parents! Today, both my step-mom and dad are a big part of my life. I'm so thankful for them! Plus, I gained two new step-brothers! How cool is that?!"

When Cody's mom married Brian, he already had two sons, Ben and Scotty. Ben is four years older than Cody, and Scotty is only three months younger than Cody. Soon after the marriage, Cody's baby stepbrother Jason was born. The four oldest brothers bonded by helping to take care of Jason. One of Cody's earliest memories is helping out with his baby brother. Cody reminisced to *BOP* magazine, "When I was still in diapers, I tried to change my younger brother's diaper, I was only two." The two families easily blended together. Scotty and Cody in particular became really good friends because they were so close in age. " . . . the person I talk to the most about everything is my step-brother Scott . . . we've been brothers since I was 2 years old . . . We're going through the same stuff all the time, so we talk to each other a lot," he told seventeen. com. Cody wasn't kidding! When Cody and Scotty were young, they each had big, purple, Barney the Dinosaur dolls. One day Cody and Scotty were having fun at the local playground with their Barney dolls in tow. Somehow, amid all the fun, Scotty's Barney doll disappeared! Even though they searched for it everywhere, they couldn't find it. So what did big brother Cody do? When he saw how sad Scotty was, he told him not to worry and gave him his own Barney doll. It was the same Barney doll that Cody slept with every night, but he didn't want his "baby bro" to be unhappy. Talk about a great brother!

When Cody's stepbrothers were around, the house was not only filled with laughter, but also lots and lots of sports equipment. Cody grew up playing soccer, football, basketball, and ice hockey with his brothers and stepbrothers. It was a good way for all the boys to bond, even if they were sometimes competitive with one other. As Cody grew older, he realized how much his two sets of parents treasured each other and how lucky he was to have twice the love from them. Cody reflected on his happy memories of his blended family and told *M* magazine, "Whatever makes your parents happy should make you happy too."

But it wasn't always fun and games at the Linley house. Even when Cody was really little, his love for silly, goofy behavior got him into trouble. Cody, like most kids, wasn't allowed to play sports in the house. But that didn't stop him from trying! Most of the time, when he and Chad attempted to play inside, they would get caught. "My brother and I got grounded for throwing a ball in our house. My mom was like, 'Don't throw the ball! If you throw the ball one more time, you're grounded for a month,'" Cody admitted to *J-14* magazine. "When she went to bed, my brother and I played this game where the ball bounced off the walls. My mom came down and grounded us for a month. It was right around Halloween and we couldn't go trick or treating."

Cody liked playing ball *outside*, too—something that his mom probably really appreciated! There were plenty of opportunities for Cody to play sports in Lewisville. There was peewee football, the Greater Lewisville Area Soccer Association, little league baseball, a track club, and the Basketball Congress International, a youth basketball league that Cody really loved. Sure, sports were fun, but Lewisville also offered something a little different that attracted Cody: a thriving arts scene. Even though Lewisville was a fairly small town, there was a Musical Feast Choral Society, the Visual Arts League, the Lewisville Symphony, the LakeCities Ballet Theatre, the Greater Lewisville Community Theatre, and the Actors Conservatory Theatre. With all those organizations in the area, it's easy to see what first inspired Cody to act. Plus, it didn't hurt that Lewisville is only a short drive from Dallas, which is a huge city. There were always different sporting events, performances, and concerts going on in Dallas, and the Linleys took advantage of it!

On top of all the cool acting organizations in Lewisville, Cody's mom Cathy, professionally known as Catherine Seymour Sullivan, was a well-known acting teacher in the area. In fact, she taught Disney starlets Demi Lovato and Madison Pettis before they were famous. She even coached Miley Cyrus twice during screentests for Miley's breakout show, *Hannah Montana*! So it's really no surprise that Cathy's children took an interest in acting. Often, when Cathy taught classes, Cody and Chad would sit in, awed by all the great performances.

In 1988, Chad had his first movie audition in Dallas. Like Los Angeles and New York City, Dallas is an important movie-making city, so that meant lots of opportunities for actors in Texas. Chad didn't book the part the first time he auditioned, but he did book a job at his second audition. It was a commercial for a Los Angeles hospital, and they filmed the spot in Nashville. That meant the family got to travel, which Cody thought was really cool. After booking his first commercial, Chad began going to auditions consistently. And when Chad went to an audition, his mom and Cody would go along. Cody, believe it or not, was a really shy kid. He kept his mom company in the waiting room, while Chad performed for the casting directors.

In December 1993, when Cody was five years old, Chad was cast as Archie Samuels, the ten-year-old half-brother to Jesse James, played by Rob Lowe, in the HBO made-for-television movie, *Frank and Jesse*. This was Cody's first glimpse of how a movie is made, and he was hooked! He dreamed of growing up to be an actor like his big brother. He wanted his chance to act with stars like Rob Lowe. Cody made the decision that he would follow in his brother's footsteps no matter what. Cody explained to shineon-media.com, "I first got into acting by my brother Chad. Once he started I wanted to follow in his footsteps."

But when Cody told his mom that he wanted to be an actor, she was hesitant to let him audition. It wasn't because she didn't think he could act. It was because, as Cody told sidewalkstv.com, "I was a really shy little boy. I don't really know what happened to me since then, but nevertheless, my mom still helped me."

When Cody wasn't accompanying Chad to auditions, they both attended Degan Elementary School. The Linley boys were very involved in school activities. Cody's favorite sport has always been basketball. He started playing for his school's team when he was in elementary school. Lucky for him, he was a natural at it! "Seventh grade, in one of my very first basketball games I played in, I shot on the buzzer at the very end and made it. Everyone went crazy! I was so happy," Cody triumphantly told *BOP* magazine. Both of the Linley boys were popular in school. Cody made friends easily, and to this day he's still good friends with many of the kids from Degan. Back then, Cody was as cute as he is now, but he had brown hair, not blond. He would dye it blond for a role much later.

Cody was definitely a cutie, even in first grade! He was popular with girls, even if he didn't always want to be. In fact, some of the girls in Cody's first grade class banded together during recess and decided to play capture the flag—with Cody as the "flag"! Cody told *M* magazine, "Every single day I would run away from them [the first grade girls]. They would never catch me because, back then I was a really fast runner. After three months I finally thought, 'I wonder what would happen if I actually let them catch me.' So that day, I ran really slow and four girls caught up to me at the same time. Then, they all kissed me on the cheek! I was like, 'Oh my gosh!' It was a pretty cool day, I must admit." That was how Cody got his very first kiss.

chapter two

A Star on the Rise

During the day, Cody and Chad went to school at Degan Elementary, but after school and on the weekends they went to Chad's auditions in Dallas and Los Angeles. It was hard work to juggle two huge responsibilites like school and auditions, but Cody and Chad always kept up with their homework. Both were very good students, but sometimes Cody got in trouble because he just couldn't sit still in class! "My worst habit is drumming on tables," he explained to seventeen.com. "I used to get in trouble in school for always drumming, talking, beat boxing and singing. But I was a pretty good student." If Cody and Chad weren't in school or playing sports with their friends, they were taking acting lessons.

Cody was preparing to start auditioning for roles. Both Linleys wanted to be the best actors they could be, so whenever they had time, they worked on their craft.

In 1995, Cody, Chad, and their mom spent six weeks in Los Angeles for pilot season. Pilot season lasts from January to April every year. It's called that because during those months television producers cast their new shows for the fall season. Every year during that time, families like the Linleys rent furnished apartments or hotel rooms in the greater Los Angeles area so their children can go to auditions for television shows. But even before pilot season that year, Chad had booked the role of Josh in *Pass the Bleachers*, an ABC made-for-television movie starring Richard Dean Anderson. This was great news, but Chad was also hoping to be cast in a new television series.

Little brother Cody was not auditioning for pilot season that year. He went to L.A. to tag along on auditions and agent meetings with his mom and Chad. Cody was only six years old, so he mostly drew pictures with crayons and played with toy cars during the meetings. Some of what he heard in those meetings must have sunk in, though, because a few years later, Cody would become an expert auditioner. Watching his brother made Cody even more excited to audition for roles when he was old enough. "It looked really fun," Cody told *Tigerbeat* magazine. When pilot season ended, Chad wasn't cast in a television show, but was up for a role in the Disney movie *Tom and Huck*. The Linleys wouldn't know if Chad had booked the role until they got back to Lewisville. Cody was inspired by his brother, and decided that soon he'd start auditioning, too.

While Cody was in fifth grade at Degan Elementary School, he got his chance to follow in Chad's footsteps: He went to his first big audition for the role of Harry Potter in the *Harry Potter* movies! Cody figured he was a long shot for the role because he wasn't British, and the casting director was leaning toward a mostly British cast. Still, Cody was probably pretty disappointed when he didn't get the part. Luckily, Cody had his mom there to help him keep it in perspective. "My mom guided me and helped me have a normal life," he told the *Dallas Morning News*. Cathy may have been an acting coach, but her job as a mom was the most important thing to her. With his entire blended family's love and support, Cody continued to learn about acting and audition for roles. Little did he know that his first break was only right around the corner.

In the following years, Cody went to so many auditions that he developed a pre-audition habit that he still sticks to today! Before auditions, Cody always stuck a very special item into his pants pocket for good luck. "I used to love Hot Wheels!" Cody told *BOP* magazine. "I would take a Hot Wheel in my pocket before I went in (to audition) for a role. Every time, I booked a movie!" His good luck started when Cody and Chad auditioned for the television movie *Still Holding On: The Legend of Cadillac Jack*. The movie starred country music singer Clint Black and his wife, actress Lisa Hartman Black. Clint Black burst onto the country music scene in his trademark black cowboy hat in 1989, and quickly became a country music superstar. Black was also an actor who appeared in movies and TV shows. He and Lisa were really affected by the true-life story of rodeo star "Cadillac" Jack Favor, so Clint and his wife decided to jump at the chance to be a part of the project.

Still Holding On: The Legend of Cadillac Jack tells the story of the wrongful murder conviction of rodeo star "Cadillac" Jack Favor. One day in 1964, the rodeo star, a native of Eula, Texas, picked up two hitchhikers. What he didn't know was that the hitchhikers had just murdered an elderly couple in Louisiana. Eventually, one of the hitchhikers was caught by the police and sent to jail. But once he's in jail, he tells the police that the cowboy Jack Favor was really the one who killed the couple. Jack travels from Texas to take a lie detector test, but when he arrives at the police station, he's arrested for the double murder! Jack's wife Ponder and his son Tommy are devastated. Ponder spends seven years trying to prove her husband's innocence, and eventually Jack is released from jail and reunited with his family.

Cody and Chad both auditioned for the role of Jack's son Tommy, and they both got it! But don't think that the Linley brothers were competing for the role: Each brother got to play Tommy at a different age! "I got to play the younger version of my brother," Cody told *Tigerbeat* magazine. This was the first time that the brothers worked together, and it was a dream come true for Cody. Talk about following in your brother's into footsteps!

Cody probably tucked his favorite Hot Wheel car into his pocket during the audition, but it was his talent that got him the role. The Linleys didn't have to travel very far to film the movie—it was filmed in their home state of Texas! All the filming was done in the towns of Cleburne, Farmersville, and McKinney. Cleburne and Farmersville were only an hour away from Cody's home, and McKinney was only thirty minutes. The Linley boys could probably film during the day and be home tucked into their own beds every night!

The movie debuted on April 28, 1998. The Linleys

most likely sat in their living room with a big bowl of popcorn and watched the two stars perform! Cody was ecstatic to see himself on the small screen, but little did he know that this was only the beginning of his bright career.

chapter three

Shining on the Silver Screen

After filming *Still Holding On: The Legend of Cadillac Jack*, Cody and Chad went back to their usual routine for a while: school, sports, acting classes, playing with the family dog Missy, and hanging out with friends. Cody also picked up another talent: He learned to play the guitar. His brothers already knew how to play, and Cody wanted to join in the fun. Cody easily learned guitar chords and had a great time looking for new music to play. "I play all the time," he told *Tigerbeat* magazine. "I love it!"

Guitar kept him pretty busy for a while, but Cody was anxious to get back out there and audition for more roles. He loved showing off his skills for casting directors and producers, but Cody didn't always get the parts he auditioned for. He told *Tigerbeat* magazine, "I've been pretty lucky, but there have been many times where I didn't get the part. I believe everything happens for a reason. It all works out in the end." Cody was right! In 1998, Cody was booked for a major motion picture called *My Dog Skip*, which released in 2000. The movie starred Kevin Bacon as Jack Morris, Frankie Muniz as Willie Morris, Diane Lane as Ellen Morris, and Luke Wilson as Dink Jenkins.

My Dog Skip takes place in the early 1940s in Yazoo City, Mississippi. The movie is based on the memoir by author Willie Morris. When Willie was a little boy, he was very shy, quiet, and introspective. He didn't have many friends and was sometimes picked on by bullies at his school. To make Willie feel better about himself, his parents bought him a terrier puppy named Skip. Skip opened up Willie's world. Through Skip, Willie was able to make friends and overcome his shyness.

Cody booked the role of Spit McGee. In the movie,

Spit starts out as one of Willie's bullies, but ends up being his friend. In fact, the real Willie Morris actually named his cat Spit McGee after his childhood friend! The character of Spit was really different from the real Cody. Spit was blond, always dirty, and was mean to his friends. The role even required Cody to walk around with a big lump of "chaw" or chewing tobacco tucked in his cheek. The real Cody couldn't have been more different—he was always kind to his friends, and he loved to shower! He once told *Tigerbeat* magazine, "I take 30-minute showers, and my mom can get ready quicker than I can! All my brothers are so quick, but I take forever to eat and get ready in the morning."

Filming the movie and playing a character so different from himself was a great experience for Cody. He loved being on set and hanging out with all the other kids who were cast in the film, especially Frankie Muniz, who played Malcolm in the hit FOX show *Malcolm in the Middle*. Plus, in 2001, Cody, Frankie Muniz, Bradley Coryell, Daylan Honeycutt, and Caitlin Wachs won the Young Artist Award for Best

Ensemble in a Feature Film. It was a huge honor for Cody because this was only his second major role!

Looking back at his first major movie experience, Cody told sidewalkstv.com, "I was lucky enough to book my first film when I was eight years old, and that was *My Dog Skip*. And from there . . . I knew, like, in my heart that acting is my dream and it's what I wanted to do for the rest of my life. My opinion about it has never changed, so I am a firm believer in pursuing your dream and doing a job that you love. Because it's awesome and it helps put you at ease, and sleep at night."

After *My Dog Skip*, Cody's next big break was guest starring on the television show *Walker, Texas Ranger.* He played the character of Timmy and acted alongside martial arts expert Chuck Norris. The show was filmed in Dallas and Fort Worth, Texas, and the set was only an hour from Cody's house. Cody first guest starred on the show in a 1999 episode, and returned in 2000 to play the role of Griffin Pope.

After some time on the small screen, Cody

auditioned for and won the role of Brownie Coop, Ashley Judd's son in the major motion picture *Where the Heart Is.* The movie was filmed in 1999 and released in 2000. Kylie Harmon plays Praline, Cody's sister, in the movie. Cody's mom in the movie, Lexie Coop, names each of her children after desserts! The movie also stars Natalie Portman, Joan Cusack, Stockard Channing, Sally Field, and Keith David. The movie is based on the best-selling novel of the same name written by Billie Letts. The movie tells the story of a pregnant seventeen-year-old, Novalee Nation, who is traveling from Tennessee to California with her boyfriend when he abandons her at a Wal-Mart in Sequoyah, Oklahoma. With only $5.55 in her pocket, Novalee lives in Wal-Mart until the birth of her child, Americus. Novalee is befriended by the townspeople of Sequoyah, including Lexie Coop. After the birth of her child, Novalee decides to live in Sequoyah and raise her child.

Where the Heart Is was also shot in the Lone Star state. The Wal-Mart that was supposed to be in

Sequoyah, Oklahoma, was actually a Wal-Mart in Lockhart, Texas. They also shot the movie in Austin, Taylor, and Waco, Texas: all easy commutes for Cody and his family. The towns of Taylor and Lockhart were less than a four-hour drive from Cody's own house.

Cody's next role on the silver screen was in the comedy *Miss Congeniality*, which was filmed and released in 2000. This movie tells the funny story of an ugly duckling, klutzy FBI agent, Gracie Hart, played by Sandra Bullock. Gracie is forced to blossom into a real beauty queen when she goes undercover as a contestant, Miss New Jersey, in the Miss United States Beauty Pageant. Their co-stars included Benjamin Bratt, Candice Bergen, William Shatner, and Sir Michael Caine. Cody didn't have a big role; in fact, Cody was only billed in the credits as "Tough Boy." In the very beginning of the movie, a young Gracie Hart breaks up a fight between two boys and punches one of them in the face. That boy was Cody! Despite his small role, Cody had a great time filming this movie, and felt lucky to be on set with such hilarious and talented co-stars. *Miss Congeniality* was filmed in Austin, Texas, where Sandra Bullock has a home, and in Round Rock and San Antonio, Texas.

Cody traveled from one set to another for his various roles. One day he'd be at home shooting hoops or strumming his guitar, or at school hanging out with his friends, and the next he'd be learning his lines on location, surrounded by talented and famous actors and actresses. Cody never let the stress he sometimes felt or the long commutes get him down. He really liked living two lives—that of a normal kid, and that of a budding star. Sure, life in front of the camera could be nerve-racking, but Cody was eating it up! Cody explained to *Teen* magazine how he felt about going on to a new set and said, "It's kind of an excited nervous. I'm usually excited to meet the director and other cast members, and anxious waiting for it to happen. But I'm never nervous that I'm going to have to work with someone weird or anything. All of my experiences in the past, everyone I've worked with has been nice and I've always had a great time on all the sets I've been on."

Cody's next role was a settler's son in the 2002 television movie *Beyond the Prairie, Part 2: The True Story of Laura Ingalls Wilder.* The movie stars Meredith Monroe as Laura Ingalls Wilder; Walter Goggins as Almanzo Wilder, Laura's husband; Skye McCole Bartusiak as Rose Wilder, Laura's daughter; Tess Harper; Lindsay Crouse; and Richard Thomas. The movie tells the story of the later part of Laura Ingalls Wilder's life, when she and her family moved to Missouri to start a new life on an apple farm. Cody played the part of Charlie Magnuson, a young friend of Laura's.

Shortly after filming was completed, Cody and his family went on a cruise to celebrate Cody's successes. That was where Cody had his first real kiss! The circumstances weren't romantic, though. One night Cody got together with a bunch of other kids on the cruise to play some games like Truth or Dare. "My first kiss happened when I was thirteen," Cody told *Twist* magazine. "It was a dare . . . and it was with a girl who was three years older than me—she was sixteen! I had no idea what I was doing. I just pretended it was NOT my first kiss, but it really was. So I was really, really nervous but I tried not to show it . . . I didn't tell her it was my first kiss."

After the cruise (and getting over the shock of his first real kiss!), Cody jumped headfirst into his next role. It was for the critically acclaimed, independent feature *When Zachary Beaver Came to Town,* which had a limited release in 2003, and won the Crystal Heart Award at the Heartland Film Festival in 2004. The movie is based on the National Book Award-winning novel by the same name written by Kimberly Willis Holt. The movie stars Jonathan Lipnicki, Eric Stoltz, and Jane Krakowski. Cody played Cal McKnight, Toby Wilson's best friend. In the movie, the two boys befriend Zachary Beaver, the fattest boy in the world. Zachary is part of a circus sideshow and gets stranded in their little Texas town when his trailer breaks down and his driver disappears.

Then, in 2003, Cody was chosen to play another bully, Quinn, who terrorizes the Baker kids in the remake of *Cheaper by the Dozen.* Steve Martin, Bonnie

Hunt, Tom Welling, Hilary Duff, Ashton Kutcher, and Piper Perabo also signed on to be a part of the cast. Cody was excited because he knew he was in the company of really great actors. Plus, it was his second movie that was filmed out of state! *Cheaper by the Dozen* was filmed in sunny California. In the movie, Steve Martin and Bonnie Hunt play a married couple, Tom and Kate Baker, who have twelve kids. The three oldest kids are Nora (Piper Perabo), Charlie (Tom Welling), and Lorraine (Hilary Duff). Tom Baker is a football coach in a small town and gets offered his dream job coaching a college football team in a big city. Tom accepts and the Baker family moves, but as they're trying to settle in, Kate leaves to go on a book tour, and Tom is left alone to look after all twelve kids. Cody plays Quinn, who makes fun of the Baker kids for not wearing the right kind of clothing.

After *Cheaper by the Dozen,* Cody had another big break. His next role, in 2004, brought him to the Disney Channel for the very first time. Cody was a guest star on the television show *That's So Raven.* The show's star, Raven-Symoné, plays a psychic teen. Her younger brother Cory Baxter is always getting into trouble, and Raven has to find a way to get him out of it. In the episode "Five Finger Discount," Cody plays Daryl, a kid who shoplifts with his friends. Daryl talks Cory into shoplifting a monkey keychain. Cory has nightmares and returns the keychain to the store. At the end of the episode, Daryl and his other shoplifting friends are caught stealing. It was a fun role for Cody to play, but it was hard for him to pretend to be a shoplifter! Cody would never steal, but luckily he was able to call on his incredible acting chops to play a convincing shoplifter.

Cody's next big movie was a perfect fit for him. He got to play a basketball player in the Martin Lawrence film *Rebound* in 2005. Martin Lawrence plays a down-and-out college basketball coach who has a problem with anger management. He ends up coaching the Mount Vernon Junior High Smelters. Patrick Warburton plays the coach of the school's rival, Vikings Junior High. Cody plays his son, Larry Burgess

Jr. There are a lot of scenes in the movie on the basketball court, which really gave Cody a chance to show off his skills. In the movie, Cody wears the Viking's purple and gold basketball uniform and makes shot after shot.

Sure, Cody had been really busy, but he knew he had to do a lot more films and television shows if he wanted to become a household name! Working with amazing actors and actresses like Martin Lawrence and Sandra Bullock was great practice, but the young star was ready to step into the spotlight. Cody may have had a lot of screen time in *Rebound*, but it was his next role that made him a leading teen star!

chapter four

Hoot, Hoot

After he finished shooting *Rebound*, Cody went home to Lewisville and back to his everyday life. Even though Cody had acted in six movies, appeared in two TV shows, and was in two made-for-television movies by the age of fifteen, he was still a normal teenage boy who liked doing all the things typical teenage boys do: playing video games, going to school, playing sports, and of course, acting silly with his friends. Cody and his friends shared the same sense of humor and loved to play pranks on each other. He talked to *J-14* magazine about some of the ways he and his friends goofed around: "My friends and I would ride elevators, and when people got in, we'd start arguments with each other to make the other people uncomfortable. Once we went to dinner and a guy we punked was at the restaurant! He applauded us, saying, 'So, you're all friends, huh?'"

Though he enjoyed the time off, Cody didn't have a ton of time to relax at home because, in 2005, his next big role came calling, and Cody couldn't turn this part down. It was the first movie where he'd be playing a starring role. The movie was *Hoot*, and Cody was tapped for the role of Mullet Fingers. Cody loved that he would be traveling out of state again for this role. The movie was filmed in southern Florida, and at one point the production was shut down because of Hurricane Katrina!

Hoot is based on Carl Hiaasen's Newbery Honor Award-winning book of the same name. Carl Hiaasen is a native Floridian who grew up in Plantation, Florida. As an adult, Hiaasen worked as a reporter for the *Miami Herald* before he became an author. Almost all of his novels are based in Florida and they almost always have a pro-environment, anti-development message in them. Cody really liked this message in *Hoot*, which was another great part about the role.

Hoot was Hiaasen's first young adult novel. *Hoot* is a classic David versus Goliath tale set in a fictionalized version of the town Coral Gables, Florida. A restaurant chain, Mother Paula's All-American Pancake House, is planning to build a new pancake house on a plot of land where endangered burrowing owls are living. But the corporation that owns the pancake house chain has managed to cover up the fact that there's an endangered species living on the land where they want to build. Only one person, a runaway teen boy who goes by the nickname Mullet Fingers, knows the truth, and he's fighting a losing battle to stop the construction. Mullet is befriended by Roy Eberhardt, played by Logan Lerman, who enlists the help of soccer star—and Mullet's stepsister—Beatrice Leep, played by the adorable actress Brie Larson. Together, the trio is determined to stop the construction and save the owls. To do it, they have to dodge police officer Delinko, played by the hilarious Luke Wilson, who is a nice but very klutzy cop, and try to prevent the construction manager Curly, played by Tim Blake Nelson, from building the restaurant on the land. In the end, the teens succeed!

Cody was happy to be reunited with Luke Wilson for this movie. A few years before, they both had roles in *My Dog Skip*. Even though Luke Wilson's star status usually means he is cast as the male lead, he really wanted to get involved in *Hoot*, despite the fact that he wasn't the main character—and he even played a bad guy! When he was interviewed by about.com, Luke explained, "I just got a call one day saying that Jimmy Buffett was doing a movie from a Carl Hiaasen book, and I mean, that right there sounded interesting to me. They were both people that I was a fan of . . . I agreed to do it before I even read the script just based on Carl Hiaasen and the book."

Music legend Jimmy Buffett was the producer of the film, but he also had a small role as the teens' science teacher—and he wrote most of the soundtrack for the movie. Jimmy's career has spanned over thirty years, but Cody wasn't aware of his musical legacy before filming the movie. As Cody explained to about.com, "I didn't know too much about his music . . . and then I told my dad, 'Hey, I'm doing a movie with Jimmy Buffett.' He's like, 'Are you serious?'"

There was a lot of excitement on and off the set, so Cody and his teen co-stars were busy even when they weren't filming. The three teens adopted three burrowing owls for the duration of the film and named them Wil, Carl, and Jimmy, after Wil Shriner, the writer/director of the movie; Carl Hiaasen, the author of the book; and Jimmy Buffett, the producer. One owl was a little bit shy, and one owl was missing a wing, but Cody loved them anyway. He told *The Movie Reporter* on IESB.net that his owl Jimmy "was calm and really cool." All three actors were given video cameras and they filmed each other playing with the owls off the set. For Cody, this was one of the best parts of working on the movie. He's always loved animals, so getting to hang out with owls all day long hardly seemed like work!

The same was true about hanging out with Luke Wilson on set. Cody and Logan had a lot of fun getting to know Luke while filming the movie. The boys took any opportunity they could to bond with the hilarious actor. The three of them even created their own game where they attempted to toss a rock through a tire hung from a tree branch fifty yards from them. Cody explained to about.com, "We didn't have a lot of scenes with him but the scenes we did, it was kind of cool because in between takes, he's kind of like a big kid . . . We were all trying to see who could hit it first, Wil would be like, 'Okay, we're rolling,' and Luke would still be throwing at the tire. We had a good time." Not only did Cody have a lot of fun with Luke, he probably learned a lot from him as well.

Both Brie and Cody and their families stayed at the Marriott Harbor Beach Hotel in Fort Lauderdale, where Cody and Brie hung out during their time off. Cody told about.com, "We had a blast on and off set. We had a rec room, which was two hotel rooms connected to each other in the hotel we were staying at that had a TV and games. We all play guitar so we'd make up this game where you made up a song."

Cody was willing to push his body to the limit for the role, even if there was danger involved. He revealed during a video interview with themovieguy.com that alligators roamed freely near where they were filming! In the movie, there's a scene where Cody is swimming in a swamp, and he explained that he was pretty nervous about it. "Yeah, it was really, really kinda scary; we saw three alligators on the way to that shot. Like a baby alligator on the rocks, and we saw a really big one underneath the water, but then where the part we were at, they had three or four scuba divers underneath there, and they had a guy with a stick to protect me from the alligators, and they were like, 'If you don't want to do it, it's totally fine,' but I really, really wanted to do it and my mom was kind of biting her nails over there, but it was really cool because we had the camera guy, the underwater camera man, was the same guy who did *Pirates of the Caribbean*."

There was plenty of danger off the set, too. On

August 23, 2005, Hurricane Katrina made landfall in southern Florida, while Cody and the rest of the cast were right in the middle of filming *Hoot*! At the time, the hurricane was a Category 1, which means that it's like a really bad rainstorm with very strong winds. Brie and Cody were told that they had to leave their hotel because it was located on the beach. On the way to their new hotel, Cody and Brie went to the supermarket and bought snacks, candles, and flashlights, thinking they could ride out the storm. Neither teen had ever been in a hurricane before and thought it couldn't be that bad. They hunkered down to wait out the storm when the hotel's fire alarms went off! Cody and Brie had to lug their guitars, luggage, and snacks down thirteen flights of stairs to safety.

Luckily, no one in the cast or crew was hurt, but not everyone was so lucky. Hurricane Katrina was one of the deadliest hurricanes in US history, and caused serious damage along the Gulf coast from Central Florida to Texas, most notably in the city of New Orleans. Almost two thousand people lost their lives due to the hurricane itself and the flooding that occurred afterward. The city of New Orleans is still rebuilding itself, and if you want to help, there are plenty of ways to volunteer, like through Katrina's Angels (katrinasangels.com). Ask a parent to help you look online for ways to help.

Hoot actually finished filming ahead of schedule, despite the problems caused by Hurricane Katrina. Overall, Cody had a great time making the movie. He told *Tigerbeat* magazine, "The most fun movie to film was *Hoot*. I was in Florida for three months with my best friend, Brie Larson." Working on *Hoot* was a great experience for Cody, but his next project would prove to be even more rewarding and exciting. Cody was about to earn some true star status with his role as the hunky Jake Ryan on the hit show *Hannah Montana*!

chapter five

Becoming Jake Ryan

Hannah Montana debuted on the Disney Channel on Friday, March 24, 2006, and instantly became a huge hit! Country singer Billy Ray Cyrus, his adorable daughter Miley, and cute actor Jason Earles, who plays Miley's older brother, had a ton of fans who tuned in each week to see what kind of wacky adventures the Stewart family would get into next. The show is centered on music. By day, Miley is just an average teenage girl, but at night she morphs into a world-famous rockstar, Hannah Montana!

When the show debuted, Cody was in Los Angeles with his family for pilot season, and one of his auditions was for a spot on an episode of *Hannah Montana*.

Cody got the part, thinking it would only be for a single episode, much like the role that he played on *That's So Raven* a few years earlier. In April 2006 during a video interview on IESB.net with *The Movie Reporter*, when asked what he would be doing next, Cody replied, "I just finished two episodes on this new Disney show called *Hannah Montana*. It's like I'm a guest star, (I have a) re-occurring role on it. This kid named Jake Ryan, who's this bigheaded TV star and I have two or three more episodes to do this season."

The character of Jake Ryan first appeared in the middle of *Hannah Montana's* first season in the episode "New Kid in School." On the show, Jake is a teen who has been famous since he was a baby. He even has his own TV show. Jake has just moved into the neighborhood and is enrolled at Seaview Middle School, the same school that Miley attends. Jake, unlike Miley, loves the star treatment he gets at school. And even though Miley works hard at hiding her other identity and usually shies away from attention, she still becomes jealous of Jake, so she almost blurts out her secret to a reporter!

Cody really liked working on the show. Off camera, the cast and crew immediately liked Cody. The producers were probably impressed with Cody's professionalism on the set, the way he got along with everyone and the fact that he and Miley clicked so well on and off the screen. So Cody was probably thrilled when his one guest-starring role morphed into a recurring one! The producers loved the idea of Jake's character on the show, and they thought Cody was a perfect fit. He was sweet, funny, and a total cutie, so they knew *Hannah Montana* fans would love him, too. Cody had great chemistry with everyone on the set; he even started to play practical jokes on other cast members! Eventually, playing practical jokes was written into the script as a part of Jake's character. And over time, Miley, Cody, and Emily became really tight buds. In an interview with *Kidsday*, Cody talked about life on the set. "*Hannah Montana* is pretty fun . . . there is a lot of fun stuff that we do on the show. I get a smoothie poured on my head. There is fighting and dancing. There is so much drama and comedy and things that we do. It is hard to narrow it down to one because everything I have done I have had a good time doing it."

Life was excellent for Cody Linley. He had a bunch of movies under his belt, and was working on a hit television show—it didn't get much better than that! But then disaster struck—Cody started to develop terrible acne. He had pimples every now and then in the past, but now it was a lot more noticeable. At first, Cody chalked it up to his teenage hormones, but when his brothers started to tease him about it, he became embarrassed. He was determined to find a quick fix, so he tried everything, even leaving toothpaste on his face overnight, a suggestion from his grandparents. Unfortunately, nothing that Cody tried seemed to work. After a while, *Hannah Montana*'s producers even approached Cody about wearing heavier stage makeup to hide his acne during the filming of the show. Cody told sidewalkstv.com, "For me, the worst time was last year, while I was doing *Hannah Montana*, whew! My face broke out really bad; it really did and that was a big deal because honestly, it was just natural, hormones. And I'm sure that the pressure and stress probably didn't help; but I was a seventeen, eighteen-year-old guy at that point. Yeah, I broke out . . . Basically I tried everything. I went to the store, I tried all these different products and nothing was working for me."

Cody finally gathered up the courage to talk to his mom about his problem, and she suggested that they go to a dermatologist. He was really glad that he was able to get over his embarrassment and confide in his mom, because her suggestion turned out to be the solution he needed. Cody's doctor prescribed medication and eventually, his acne went away.

Cody was relieved, but started to think that there were probably a lot of other teens out there with the same problem, who maybe weren't lucky enough to get help from a doctor. He tried to think of ways to reach out to them, and discovered Acne Heroes (acneheroes.com). The organization was happy to have Cody as a spokesperson, and he was happy to help. Cody told seventeen.com, "[The website] clears up all the myths about acne, like, 'Oh yeah, if you wash your face five times a day then you'll be five times cleaner,' or 'If you eat chocolate it's going to cause breakouts.' You know, you've heard them and some of them you're like, 'I didn't eat that much chocolate because I thought it might be true!' It clears all that stuff up." Besides being a spokesperson, Cody also got involved with the organization's Clearly Spirited Heroes Challenge. The grand prize was a visit at your school from none other than Cody Linley himself! Cody loved that he was able to help other teens going through the same things he went through. Don't worry if you get acne someday— you can visit the Acne Heroes website for answers, or talk to your parents about it. Just don't try the toothpaste trick—Cody knows better than anyone else that it doesn't work!

Once his acne was under control, Cody could concentrate 100 percent on his role as Jake Ryan on *Hannah Montana*. The show's loyal fans couldn't get enough of Cody; they loved him from the moment they first saw him strolling through the halls of Seaview

Middle School as the cocky but adorable Jake Ryan. For most of his life, Cody had been just a regular kid who acted in movies while he wasn't in school. Now, he was a superstar! Needless to say, he was overwhelmed by all the love and attention from fans. When shineonmedia.com asked Cody what his reaction was to all the attention from *Hannah Montana*'s legions of fans, his only reply was, "Wow. Wow. Wow. I had no idea how powerful the Disney Channel is."

When the producers saw the fans' response to Cody, they knew they had to have him back for seasons two and three—and, of course, Cody said yes! He was having the time of his life. He even told *Twist* magazine, "I'm really thankful that I've been lucky enough to land such a great role like playing Jake Ryan on *Hannah Montana*!"

In between filming episodes of *Hannah Montana*, Cody flew back to Texas to go to school. But when Cody was in Los Angeles for the show's filming, he enrolled in Options for Youth, an independent school program for teen actors. It was important to Cody to keep up with his schoolwork, and to make sure he was studying the same things his classmates back home were studying. Cody was still getting used to all the travel involved with filming in L.A.—it was a lot easier when the Linley family could drive to Cody's film sets! Once Cody's first *Hannah Montana* episode aired, life started to change at light speed. Before, Cody's friends and classmates treated him like he was a regular kid, but now that he was a star on their favorite TV show, everyone at school and in his small town treated him like a superstar. He talked about these big changes to disneysociety.com. "When I'm not filming a TV show or a movie, I am back home, which is a town near Dallas, Texas. I go to public school when I'm there. Before *Hannah Montana*, I didn't really get recognized a lot. Every once in a while, people would come up to me and say, 'Have you been in a movie because I swear I've seen you somewhere' . . . At my school a friend of mine is this big guy. He came up to me and was like, 'My sister was watching you on Disney and I saw four of your episodes.' and I was like, 'You watch Disney?'

He was like, 'I was just flipping the stations!'"

Pretty soon, fans started to approach Cody to ask him for his photo, and he always said yes with a smile. "A fan came up to me and I was like, 'do you want a picture?'" he told *Tigerbeat* magazine. "She handed me the camera to take a picture of her and then took the camera and left . . . that was very odd." What was even odder for Cody was when he went to a high school football game and was chased by fifty people with cameras trying to take his picture!

Even though Cody was becoming more famous, he stayed grounded and his irrepressible sense of fun kept him upbeat. "Why be normal? Goofy is more fun!" Cody told *M* magazine. "I like to make up funny dances to songs by Britney Spears and the Backstreet Boys. My friends and I are total goofballs. We like to rap and make up crazy dances. Seriously, we'll just bust out rapping anywhere! It's funny to see people's reactions when we start doing it. Some people get scared and don't know what to make of us. But then others will think we're actually cool and give us the thumbs up! A few times, people have started dancing with us. I usually don't rap for a girl when I first meet her though. Most girls aren't that into goofy guys!"

Cody was lucky that his guy friends were true buds, and didn't change how they acted around him no matter how famous he became. Cody told *J-14* magazine about a time that he was recognized at the movies and his friends came through for him. "A bunch of girls started pointing at me, when that happens, my friends have a code *HM* alert for *Hannah Montana*. I hide in the restroom until my friends come and gather all around to sneak me into the theater." Most of the time, though, Cody loves to meet his fans and sign autographs for them. "I love having the opportunity to make someone happy," he proudly told *J-14* magazine.

Cody stayed close with all his best friends from Texas even as he became tight with his *Hannah Montana* co-stars Emily Osment and Miley Cyrus. Both Emily and Miley shared Cody's wild sense of humor, so the three of them really bonded. At first, Miley even had a bit of a crush on Cody. She told *M* magazine, "He's so perfect. Too bad he doesn't like me. I wish he did. On *Hannah Montana* his character is really lovey-dovey with mine, but in real life he doesn't feel that way about me at all! I did get to kiss him for the show though. Best kisser in the entire world! His lips are perfect. I look at him and go 'Ahh, he's gorgeous!'" Cody and Miley kept their romance on-screen, and were just close friends off-screen. Cody told *Twist* magazine, "We're really, really good friends . . . just a week ago, I was over her house and we were swimming and stuff."

Cody and Emily quickly became close friends as well. Cody loved to prank call her pretending to be Borat, Sasha Baron Cohen's character from the movie *Borat*. When Emily and Cody had downtime on the *Hannah Montana* set, the two of them loved to play ping-pong! Cody told *M* magazine, "I loved playing ping pong on breaks with Emily. She's a tough competitor! I rooted for her to win this summer during the *DC Games*." Cody and Emily loved playing games together on the set. It was probably great practice for Cody's next adventure: the Disney Channel Games!

chapter six

On the Other Side of the Mic

In 2008, between filming episodes of *Hannah Montana*, Cody, Miley Cyrus, Emily Osment, Mitchel Musso, Moises Arias, and other Disney stars from across the globe flew to Orlando, Florida, to participate in the Disney Channel Games hosted by Brian Stepanek. The five-day, Olympics-style event was held at Disney World. It was a fun way for the stars to get to know one other, and for fans to see all of their favorite actors and actresses together in one place. But before the competition even began, Cody was assigned an extra-special job. He and Meaghan Jette Martin from *Camp Rock* were asked to host an online show called *Inside Track* that covered all the behind-the-scenes stuff that was going on. Cody and Meaghan had a blast interviewing other Disney stars throughout the games. Cody was a natural interviewer. He knew how to make his interviewees, like Cole Sprouse and Mitchel Musso, laugh and have a great time while answering questions, a trick that takes years for some talk show hosts to learn! Plus, the fans loved it.

One of Cody's interviews was with Jason Dolley from the Disney show *Cory in the House*. Jason is a bonafide hottie, just like Cody, and some people even think they look alike! Cody told Jason, "Just yesterday I got asked if I was Jason Dolley." Jason responded, "And two days ago, I was asked if I was Cody Linley. I just kept walking. I was like I don't know what to do here!" The boys laughed, and spent the rest of the interview comparing heights, and trying to figure out if they looked alike from the back. The fans adored it! Cody also interviewed the gorgeous actress Selena Gomez from the show *Wizards of Waverly Place*. Cody asked Selena a series of "rapid-fire" questions, and when he asked her what her favorite place in the world was, Selena replied, "Texas." Then the two native Texans gave each other a high five.

A fan-favorite interview was with the Jonas Brothers, the adorable Grammy-nominated trio of brothers. Cody loves to rap, and he actually got the three brothers to freestyle rap while he beatboxed along with them! Cody's interviews were so popular with fans, that if he ever decides to stop acting, he could probably have a career as a talk show host! Cody was so busy interviewing other Disney stars that he wasn't able to participate in the games himself, but he loved watching all his friends go head-to-head in zany competitions—like Foos It or Lose It, a human foosball match—and then interviewing them about it.

During the games, the stars were divided into four teams. The Cyclones/Green Team was headed up by captain Davis Henrie, and team members included Jason Dolley, Clara Alonso (from Argentina), Joe Jonas, Brad Kavanagh, Ambra Lo Faro (from Italy), Dylan Sprouse, Chelsea Staub, and Jennifer Stone. The Comets/Yellow Team had Kevin Jonas as captain and his team members included Moises Arias, Martin Barlan (from France), Sabrina Ryan, Yi Chun (from Taiwan), Selena Gomez, Andrea Guasch (from Spain), Kyle Massey, and Kunal Sharma (from India). The Inferno/Red Team featured Brenda Song as the captain, and also included Jake T. Austin, Deniz Akdeniz (from Australia), Adrienne Bailon, Rafa Baronesi (from Brazil), Jason Earles, Nick Jonas, Mitchel Musso, Ana Maria Pcrez de Tagle, and Jasmine Richards. And finally, the Lightning/Blue Team included Kiely Williams as captain and Farez Bin Juraimi (from Singapore), Roshon Fegan, Roger Gonzalez (from Mexico), Shin Koyamada, Demi Lovato, Isabella Soric (from Germany), Cole Sprouse, and Alyson Stoner.

The four teams participated in fun challenges like running through obstacle courses, guessing each other's baby pictures, and other games. The Jonas Brothers, Miley Cyrus, the Cheetah Girls, Demi Lovato, and Jordan Pruitt all performed musical acts. In the end, the Red Team won the competition with 100 points, though the Yellow Team was close behind them with 70. The Blue and Green Teams tied with 55 points each. Various awards were handed out to the contestants. Selena Gomez won a Fan Favorite award for looking most like her baby picture, and Dylan Sprouse won an award for being the most competitive. And Cody was there every step of the way to record the zaniness for Disney fans worldwide! Disney fans who didn't know Cody from *Hannah Montana* got to know him through his adorable online videos with all their favorite stars.

After the games, Cody went straight to work on season two of *Hannah Montana*. That season ran from April 23, 2007, through October 12, 2008, featured thirty new episodes, and even featured guest appearances by Dwayne "The Rock" Johnson and Heather Locklear. This was also the season when Moises Arias became a regular cast member. Two of Cody's biggest highlights in this season were the episodes "Achy Jakey Heart, Part One" and "Achey Jakey Heart, Part Two." These episodes focus on Miley and Jake's relationship, and in the second one, Jake even creates a "normal person" disguise to try to blend in. It's the opposite of Miley's Hannah Montana superstar disguise! After the season wrapped, the cast and crew threw a huge party to celebrate a successful two years. Cody recorded his happy memories of this night on his official blog, codymlinley.com. "Then tonight I went to the *Hannah Montana* Season Two Wrap party. It was really fun. It was a casino-themed party so I got $500 of fake money to gamble with when I got there. I lost all my money eventually :(but it was really fun. I taught Emily Osment how to play poker, craps and roulette. SHE won a lot of money! It was cool seeing the whole cast and crew. We watched the blooper reel of Season 2 that was really funny. They had the scene in the episode 'Achy Jakey Heart, Part 2' where [Miley] puts a whole bunch of ice cream in my mouth to shut me up. We did a lot of takes where she put a huge scoop of ice cream in my mouth over and over again and she couldn't keep from laughing."

And while the party seemed like the perfect end to

a great year, the best was yet to come. That year the teen cast of *Hannah Montana* was nominated for the 2008 Young Artist award for Best Ensemble Performance in a TV Series. Cody Linley's star was rising: There was no looking back for this teen heartthrob!

chapter seven

Thrills and Chills

Cody knew that with big success, also came big sacrifices. He was lucky that up to this point, he could still go to school with his friends in Texas, play on the basketball team, and hang out with his brothers while they all jammed on their guitars. But traveling back and forth between Texas and Los Angeles became harder and harder for Cody and his parents, so eventually, he knew he'd have to give up something that he loved. But for Cody, that wasn't going to be acting—instead, he had to give up his second love, playing basketball, so he had more time to perfect his craft. "I was on my school's basketball team for a long time," he told *Twist* magazine, "But when I decided that I really

CRAZY
FOR CODY

Cody flashes a smile for the cameras at the
High School Musical 2 premiere.

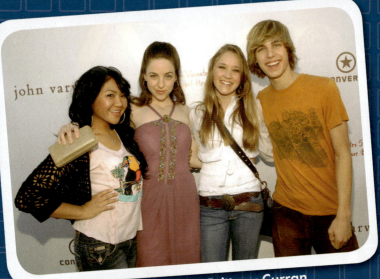

Disney friends Mallory Low, Brittany Curran, Emily Osment, and Cody Linley.

Cody and his *Dancing with the Stars* partner Julianne Hough bust a move on the "purple" carpet.

Cody and Julianne Hough pose for pictures at the Los Angeles premiere of *High School Musical 3*.

Cody looking tough at the CMA awards.

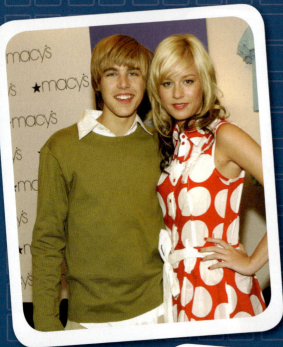

Cody and his *Hoot* co-star Brie Larson at the movie's premiere in 2006.

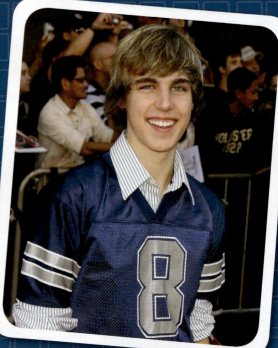

Cody shows his Texas pride.

wanted to pursue acting I had to choose. I had to come to LA last February and that's right around when the playoffs are, right at the end of the season, so I knew I just couldn't do both. I like playing basketball, but I like being an actor more. My passion has always been acting. I want to pursue it as my career forever. I love, love, love it! It's an opportunity that not many people have a chance to explore."

Cody's budding love life was also affected by the choice he made to devote most of his time to acting. Cody broke up with his then-girlfriend, even though he really liked her, because he wasn't in Texas enough of the time. " . . . I definitely had to split with a girl because the timing wasn't right . . . It can stink sometimes because I really liked the girl and she liked me . . ." Cody told *M* magazine.

Though he was now spending most of his time in L.A., Cody wouldn't let the time he spent in Texas be "downtime." He continued to work on his acting at home by helping out at his mom's acting studio, Everybody Fits, in Coppel, Texas. Cody's duties included teaching improv classes and coaching young actors. When he wasn't in Los Angeles, Cody would often teach classes five times a week.

As if his schedule wasn't busy enough, Cody managed to find time to squeeze in a few side projects in between filming *Hannah Montana* and helping out at his mom's studio. In one of them, Cody was cast as Sean, and fellow *Hannah Montana* castmate Emily Osment was cast as Cassie, in R.L. Stine's *The Haunting Hour: Don't Think About It,* a film that came out in 2007. It was Cody's first scary movie, and it was a great role for the young star. An evil monster is on the loose and Sean has to protect his friends: Cassie, a goth girl who's just moved into the neighborhood; her brother Max, played by Alex Wizenread; Priscilla, the most popular girl at school, played by super-cute Brittany Curran; and a Papa John's Pizza delivery man. Cody told *Teen* magazine, "It was my first time to ever go on a movie already knowing someone on set. Usually I go in and meet a whole bunch of new people, but this was cool. [Emily and I] hung out off set a lot and played games, threw a football around. She's kind of a tomboy, which is good because I have four brothers and I don't have any sisters, so I'm used to doing guy stuff. But Brittany Curran, on the other hand, is a real girly girl. I was friends with her too, and we all hung out together, but I have to say Emily is better at sports than Brittany."

The three teens got the chance to bond over more than just sports. Because the movie was filmed in the fall, Cody, Emily, and Brittany had the opportunity to celebrate Halloween together. " . . . Brittany, Emily, and I went to a haunted house," Cody told *Teen* magazine. "I am not really into haunted houses that much because I don't want to be scared. But they dragged me along and it was pretty funny because Brittany was on my left and Emily was on my right side, and they were grabbing my arms. We walked through this haunted house and they were screaming and I was trying to act like I wasn't scared, but I was as scared as they were. It was really fun, because we were laughing at each other because I got scared and they were laughing at me." Pretty funny that these actors were scared of a haunted house and not of the terrifying movie they were shooting together!

The movie was filmed in Pittsburgh, Pennsylvania, which gets really cold in the fall. Cody's fans would sometimes stand for three hours at a time in the cold just waiting to say hello to him. Cody told *BOP* magazine, "There were 25 girls who had this gigantic banner that said, 'We Love You Cody!' I thought that was really cool of them." Cody loves his fans, so he stopped to say hello and sign autographs and take pictures with them. He told *BOP* magazine, "I even signed a couple of heads!"

Cody's other side project was a little bit different, but still just as cool. He had the chance to be the voice of Joe Hardy in *The Hardy Boys: The Hidden Theft,* a computer video game based on the famous mystery novels for boys. He was cast alongside singer Jesse McCartney, who voiced Joe's brother Frank. The game was created by the Adventure Company. The characters' animation was based on Cody and Jesse's looks, so the video game characters are just as cute as the real guys! The game was released to the public on September 30, 2008, amid a lot of excitement and fanfare.

The Hardy Boys Mystery Stories first debuted in 1927, and the books have been popular since then. The series stars two teenage brothers who become amateur detectives after watching their dad, a real detective, hard at work. The stories were spun off into live action and animated television series. Cody probably read the books himself when he was younger!

Cody was interviewed on the Adventure Company's website about his experience voicing such a well-known character. "Playing Jake Ryan on *Hannah Montana*—it's been like a crazy experience—it's changed my life. So playing Joe Hardy is like playing a classic character that has been around for so long compared to *Hannah Montana* which is something that has been a recent success. It's really cool. It's fun for me because as an actor, I like to play different characters and characters opposite of me, so to play two very different characters is fun. Really fun." He continued, "And the cool thing about the Hardy Boys too, is that there's lots of action adventure along with it, and that's rare for roles for kids like me. There's running around, driving in cars, doing all kinds of cool things, solving mysteries that you don't really see. The Hardy Boys is so original, there's nothing else like it really."

There are five more Hardy Boys video games planned for the future. The Adventure Company hasn't yet announced whether or not they'll continue to use Cody and Jesse as voice actors for the series, but fans would love it if they did! At age eighteen, Cody had already been a star on the big screen and the small screen, and was made into a video game character! But pretty soon, Cody would face another challenging role: dancer!

chapter eight

Dancing
with Cody

The year 2008 was a really big one for Cody. He graduated high school in the spring, and packed up and moved to Los Angeles with his two best buds from Lewisville. Now the young star could concentrate full-time on his career. For fun, Cody and his friends played basketball, went to the mall, saw movies, and played video games. Sometimes Cody would hang out with another Disney star, Roshan Fegan, and rap. But the one thing that Cody never seriously attempted to do was any type of dancing.

Even when he was back home in Lewsville, and went to school dances, Cody really didn't dance with girls because he was shy. It was easy for him to make up funny dances, but slow dancing for Cody—or any teen guy, for that matter—was always a painful experience. Cody always had trouble figuring out where to put his arms and how fast to move his feet during a slow dance. But all that was about to change in a big way! Cody had no idea that shortly after he made his move to Los Angeles, he'd learn how to ballroom dance with one of the prettiest and sweetest dancers from *Dancing with the Stars*!

Dancing with the Stars is a popular television show on ABC that pairs a celebrity from the sports, music, acting, or singing industries with a professional ballroom dancer. The "regular" celebrities have to master complicated ballroom dances like the quickstep, rumba, samba, paso doble, and even the waltz. After performing live in front of a studio audience, they're given scores by the TV judges: Carrie Ann Inaba, Len Goodman, and Bruno Tonioli. Then viewers vote for their favorite pairs by calling, texting, or going online to the *DWTS* website. The pair with the lowest combined scores between the viewers and the judges is eliminated each week. This happens every week for ten weeks until only one couple remains, and they're crowned the champions! Past celebrities who have appeared on the *DWTS* stage are Olympians Apollo Ohno (speed skating) and Kristi Yamaguchi (ice-skating), actors Mario Lopez and Monique Coleman, and singers Mel B and Billy Ray Cyrus. Every contestant on the show wears really elaborate dance costumes—that goes for the men, too. And everyone also wears thick stage makeup so that the bright studio lights won't wash the contestants' complexions out. In fact, *Dancing with the Stars* uses 150 gallons of spray-tan each season!

When Cody was first approached to be a contestant on *Dancing with the Stars*, he was hesitant to say yes. He was nervous about dancing in front of a live studio audience, and a potential fifteen weeks was an awfully long time to dedicate to one thing he wasn't even sure he was good at. Cody has always been a natural athlete, which meant he was quick on his feet, but could that transition from the basketball court to a ballroom?

Cody even told *TV Guide*, "What do I know about dancing? I played basketball, football, ice hockey and soccer!" But in the end, Cody decided to go for it and take on this new challenge. He told the *Fort Worth Star-Telegram* that he decided, "I could learn to dance, and I like to learn new stuff, so why not, let's do it." Cody never backed down from a challenge, and this was his most exciting challenge yet. Even though he was a little scared, he decided to take the plunge, and hoped that his fans would show him a ton of support. He didn't know at the time that he would gain even *more* fans by the end of the show!

Rehearsals started five weeks before opening night. Cody was partnered with Julianne Hough. At the time, Julianne happened to be the youngest professional dancer on *Dancing with the Stars*. Adorable Julianne was born on July 20, 1988, which made her only a year older than Cody. It was perfect that the two young stars got to work together, and Cody was less intimidated because he got to work with someone his own age. Julianne's older brother Derek is also a professional dancer who appears on *DWTS*, so dancing definitely runs in her blood. In fact, Julianne had already been a two-time winner of *Dancing with the Stars* in past seasons. Cody knew he had an excellent teacher, and even told *People* magazine, "A lot of people are saying, 'You've got the best partner so you better step up your game!'"

The two got along really well. "She's exactly who I wanted to be my partner. I am very lucky. We're both determined, young and we like to have fun," Cody told *In Touch Weekly*. "My roommates are jealous." During the hours-long rehearsals, the two would joke around and laugh a lot while working on dance steps. "We have a similar sense of humor," Cody told *Us* magazine. "One of us will burp and we'll crack up!" Julianne may have been Cody's partner in crime some of the time, but she also insisted that he work his hardest for the show. Part of this was learning to eat healthy foods and getting into excellent shape. Cody cut out Cap'n Crunch cereal and frozen DiGiorno pizza from his diet, and added fruit and health bars to balanced meals. In addition to dancing, Cody started lifting weights for an hour each day. He told the *Dallas Morning News*, "I had no idea it would be as intense as it is. But it's a good thing. I've gotten in great shape."

Cody was truly focused on becoming the best dancer he could be, but that didn't mean he ignored his other responsibilities. He went to dance rehearsals during the day, and at night went home and memorized scripts for the upcoming season of *Hannah Montana*. Cody's roommates would sometimes ask him how he was holding up, and he would reply with a smile. "I'm like, 'I was dancing with Julianne all day,' and they're like, 'I hate you man!'" Cody told *In Touch Weekly*. Not a bad way to spend a day!

During rehearsals, Julianne and Cody danced for ten hours a day, seven days a week. Cody told *People* magazine, "The first couple of weeks I got really sore . . . in parts of my body that I never knew had muscles! Like the inside of my legs? I never expected that to hurt." When he wasn't in rehearsals with Julianne, Cody also had dancing help from his *Hannah*

Montana co-star and on-screen girlfriend Miley Cyrus, and her dad Billy Ray Cyrus. Billy Ray was a former *DWTS* contestant, so he gave Cody pointers—and even gave him a special shirt to wear during dance rehearsals. Cody told *E!* Online, "[Billy Ray] gave me some pointers, actually, and every time I see him he always asks me about the dancing . . . he said that I'm going to have the greatest time but it's also very scary. And I said, 'all right! Bring it on!'" Cody and Miley practiced dance moves during breaks on the set of *Hannah Montana*. Cody told *E!* Online that there were times when he'd go over to Miley, and say, ". . . 'We got to practice this,' and we'd be dancing, and I'd, like, dip her, and she'd be like, 'Ok, that's enough. I'm not Julianne, and I'm not doing that!'" But Miley's a good friend, so then they'd go back to practicing minus the dips!

At first, it probably seemed to Cody like the premiere of the show would never arrive. But before long, it was Monday, September 22, 2008—the first night of the seventh season of *Dancing with the Stars*.

Season seven featured thirteen couples, the most competitors ever on the show. Cody was up against volleyball Olympic gold medalist Misty May-Treanor, Olympian Maurice Greene, NFL champion Warren Sapp, singers Lance Bass and Toni Braxton, actors Ted McGinley, Susan Lucci, and Chloris Leachman (who was eighty-two years old, the oldest *DWTS* contestant to appear on the show!), television personalities Kim Kardashian and Brooke Burke, chef Rocco DiSpirito, and comedian Jeffrey Ross. Season seven was also the first time that the first three episodes were aired back-to-back, which meant a double elimination during the first week! After that, the show went back to its regular, but still stressful, routine: Monday night was competition night and Tuesday night was results night. Cody would be dancing live twice every week. The pressure was on, and he knew it.

Backstage at Studio 46 at CBS Television City in Los Angeles, on that first Monday night of the show, all the contestants and their dance partners were dressed and ready to go. They were all psyched to show the packed studio audience, and TV viewers watching worldwide, what they had been practicing so hard. The lights went down, the theme music blared from the speakers, and the show began!

Cody and Julianne were the first couple to make their grand entrance down the staircase—which also meant they were the first couple to dance that night. Talk about nerves! Cody and Julianne's first dance was the cha-cha. After it was over, Cody and Julianne stood breathlessly before the judges, waiting to hear what their verdict would be. All three judges were very enthusiastic in their praise. Judge Len Goodman told them, "You came out full of confidence. It was high-energy dancing . . . great job." In the end, the judges gave the couple a combined total 18 points. That was probably enough to keep them safe from that week's double elimination, as long as their score from the following night was just as good. Cody knew after just one night that he loved being a part of *Dancing with the Stars.* He told *Us* magazine how he felt when he hit the stage: "I'm not going to lie—I was pretty nervous! We kicked it off, so I had lots of butterflies, but we did have a blast out there!"

On the very next night, Cody and Julianne performed the quickstep to the song "I Want You to Want Me" by Letters to Cleo. Cody wore a dashing, black tuxedo and looked like an old-fashioned movie star, and Julianne wore a gorgeous, flame-red gown adorned with sequins. After they finished dancing, the pair gave each other a high five. They deserved it, too—they had blown the judges away! Judge Bruno Tonioli burst out saying, "Kings and queen of the proms! Your parents must be so proud! I was! . . . What charm and energy! . . . A little bit more control and you'll get even better." Judge Carrie Ann Inaba even said, "I think, Cody, you have gone from being a boy to a man on the ballroom dance floor!" That night they were awarded 23 points by the judges, which, combined with their score from the previous night, was enough to keep them safe from elimination. On the elimination show the very next night, comedian Jeffrey Ross and actor Ted McGinley were each eliminated. The audience was also entertained that night with performances by Cody's friends, Jesse McCartney and the Jonas Brothers.

The following week, Cody and Julianne danced the rumba. But before their dance, the show's producers aired a video of Julianne teaching Cody the moves—and, of course, it showed the two of them goofing around. After the video, the show went live, and the dashing couple danced the rumba to "Bleeding Love," wearing complementary, sparkly, gold and white outfits. Just like the week before, Cody and Julianne blew the judges away! Judge Len Goodman told the audience, "Avert your eyes, because this boy's on fire. Good job! Well done!" The judges gave the pair a combined score of 21 points, which was enough to keep them safe from elimination for another week. On the next show, relaxed and feeling loose, Cody and Julianne danced the jive. They prepared themselves for a possible elimination, but then they got some news. Misty May-Treanor announced she had to drop out of the competition due to an injury. It was especially disappointing because it meant that week's scores would be added to the following week's scores for one results show. Cody and Julianne would have to be perfect.

For week four, Cody and Julianne performed the tango. Cody was really nervous about this one, and not just because of the impending elimination show—his friend Emily Osment was also in the audience! Cody's nerves showed on the stage. He accidentally stepped on Julianne's hem a few times during the dance because her outfit was so big and flowy! But it didn't matter, because the judges still applauded their performance. Bruno told Cody that it looked like he was "starting to find [his] mojo!" Cody was thrilled to hear Len say, "the little boy has turned into the boy wonder tonight . . . your best dance so far." Cody and Julianne receieved 23 points that night, and combined with the previous week's score and the audience's votes, it was enough to keep them safe from elimination!

The very next week, Cody and Julianne performed the jitterbug. The pair did such an excellent job that Bruno, who is known for being tough on contestants, told the duo, "That wasn't a jitterbug, that was a firebug!" Carrie Ann said, " . . . that was the perfect dance for you." And Len Goodman told them, "Well, it had fun, it was entertaining, it had energy. I liked it very much!" The judges gave them 28 points. So far that was the pair's highest score, which should have been a reason to celebrate, but the audience started to boo! The audience thought that Cody and Julianne deserved an even *higher* score. Cody started to think that he had a shot at winning the competition. The fans sure thought so!

A special guest judge, Michael Flatley, famous for creating *Riverdance* and *Lord of the Dance*—shows that feature Celtic dance, appeared on the show the next week. Cody should have been excited, but he had gotten some bad news. Julianne had appendicitis, and had to drop out of the show for a while to recover. In fact, she had to have surgery, so that night's dance, the samba, and the following night's dance at the elimination show would be her last for a while. Cody was probably bummed to be losing his partner, but he was probably very concerned about her, too!

After Julianne left the show, Cody would be dancing with Edyta Sliwinska. Edyta, like Julianne, is one of the show's professional dancers, and has been with *Dancing with the Stars* for a few seasons. She had been eliminated during the first week of the competition with her partner, comedian Jeffrey Ross. Now, Edyta was back, determined to step in for Julianne and help Cody win the competition.

Cody and Julianne danced amazingly well that night. Cody probably turned up the heat because he knew that it was one of his last dances with Julianne for a while. Everyone was so impressed with Cody's skills that the host, Tom Bergeron, turned to Julianne and said, "You've created a monster!" It was official: Cody was a dancing fiend! The judges all praised the couple for their intense samba, and Flatley even said, "I think the best is yet to come from you." The judges gave the pair 23 points. The next night, Cody and Julianne danced a beautiful tango for the elimination show, and then said a tearful good-bye. Cody told usmagazine.

com, "I'm bummed that Julianne is gone . . . My love and support and prayers go to her, and I'm going to be there to support her through this whole thing. But I know she's going to be OK, and hopefully [she'll] be back to dance with me again next week if I'm still around . . . I'm dancing with Edyta and I'm excited about that, because she's an awesome dancer." Cody did, in fact, stick around, so it was on to week eight, and a new partner.

Cody and Edyta's first dance together was a waltz. But before they hit the stage, a video aired of the two of them visiting Julianne in the hospital and practicing their moves for her. Julianne's fans must have loved that! Cody dedicated his dance that week to Julianne, and he and Edyta set the stage on fire. The audience went wild with applause—it seemed that Cody was just as good with a brand-new partner. Len told them, "I thought as a couple you looked really comfortable together." The judges gave Cody and Edyta a total of 22 points, which wasn't what Cody's fans in the audience were hoping for. The couple could have been eliminated, but the home audience took to their phones and computers and voted for Cody and his partner, so they were safe yet again.

Cody was relieved, but he didn't have much time to relax after that. The next morning he appeared on two different local television shows for interviews. He wore a white jacket over a fitted black T-shirt and a trendy dog tag necklace around his neck. One of the interviews was with *My Fox–LA*, where Cody seemed really relaxed and happy. When he was asked how he kept himself grounded, Cody replied, "Well, it's been ridiculously crazy. Every day is a completely new learning experience for me. I mean, I'm eighteen years old, I moved out to L.A. just about four, five months ago. And now like with *Dancing with the Stars*, I'm learning a new dance, I'm on TV, live in front of twenty million people, been just an amazing experience and I'm just trying to enjoy the experience and have fun with it, and also get as many votes as I can, because last night wasn't the best night for me on *Dancing with the Stars* . . . I'm so absorbed in *Dancing with the Stars*. I rehearse every day for seven hours a day, like seven to eight hours a day. Right after this, I'm going to rehearse with Edyta from eleven to five . . . because we need every day that we can. It's a seven-day work schedule. It's kinda hectic and crazy, but it's also the most exciting thing I've ever done."

This kind of crazy schedule was becoming routine for Cody. He was used to interviewing in the morning, and rehearsing for the rest of the day. After all, it was week seven of *Dancing with the Stars*, which meant it was crunch time. Only two more weeks remained before the finals, and only five couples were left!

Week eight was especially tough because each pair had to master two different dances, one of which featured a fifteen-second solo. Cody was lucky enough to have the support of his friends and family during this nerve-racking time. During dance rehearsals with Edyta, Cody's buds, including Roshon Fegan, a rapper also known for his role in Disney's *Camp Rock*, dropped by to say hello and offer support. Cody's friends met Edyta and watched the pair dance—Ro even tried to steal Edyta away for a dance. The producers of *DWTS* caught it all on tape for the home audience, and the fans loved it. Cody and Edyta were the first to dance on week eight's episode, and they did an excellent foxtrot. The talented couple looked like a modern day Fred Astaire and Ginger Rogers. The audience applauded non-stop during their routine, and Ro and Cathy Sullivan, Cody's mom, were the audience members cheering the loudest. The judges gave the duo 24 points. But Cody couldn't relax just yet—he had another dance to perform that night.

Cody and Edyta's second dance was a mambo, and was the dance in which Cody had to perform a fifteen-second solo. Cody thrilled the audience with a high airborne split that transitioned flawlessly back into his steps. Cody danced his solo with energy and grace, and ended it all with a bang by leaping onto the judges' table! The studio audience gave Cody and his partner a standing ovation, and even the host said, "Great stuff!" Judge Carrie gave Cody an "A for effort, A for energy." The judges all agreed that it was a strong performance, but felt a little erratic at times. They awarded the couple 24 points, for a combined score of 48 for the night. Then Cody got the best news of all: Julianne would be coming back to dance with Cody the next night during the results show, and would continue to be his partner from there on out! The next night, Julianne returned to the stage amid a lot of cheers and applause, and Cody was thrilled to hear that he was safe from elimination!

The next week flew by. It was now week nine of *Dancing with the Stars*, and only four couples remained: Lance Bass and Lacey Schwimmer, Brooke Burke and Julianne's brother Derek, Warren Sapp and Kym Johnson, and, of course, Cody and Julianne. Cody knew he was at the bottom of the pack and needed to work really hard on his next two dances, the salsa and the paso doble, if he wanted to stay in the competition. He was so excited that Julianne was back, though, and told the *Fort Worth Star-Telegram*, "It's awesome that Julianne's back. She's amazing. We had so much momentum and chemistry built up during the competition, and then she had her surgery. But now, with two weeks of rest, she's back, and she is excellent and ready to dance."

Despite his excitement, Cody's first dance of week nine's competition was disappointing. The judges thought the couple looked stiff, and gave them only 22 points. Cody and Julianne had one more chance to prove themselves. For their salsa number, the couple wore adorable, bright yellow outfits and danced to fun, upbeat music. Cody even got to lift and twirl Julianne in the air. They were having a ton of fun, but was it enough to keep them in the competition? The judges gave the dancers decent critiques, and 24 points, which meant a total of 46 points. That put Cody and Julianne in last place. If Cody wanted to stay on the show, it was entirely up to the fans to vote him into the next round.

The next night, Tuesday, November 18, one day before Cody's nineteenth birthday, Cody and Julianne put their dancing shoes back on for the most nerve-racking results show they'd faced so far. The lineup of musical guests that night was amazing—there were performances by the legendary Aretha Franklin and adorable Brit sensation Leona Lewis. Cody was too nervous to really enjoy it, though. In between songs, the host asked the judges their thoughts about the remaining couples. Of course, the first contestant the judges spoke about was fan-favorite Cody. Len Goodman said, "Well, you know what I love about Cody is that he gives one hundred ten percent! He's enthusiastic, he's got a great work ethic, and the ladies at the grocer's tell me he's cute!"

After the judges spoke, a video montage played of all the contestants' families. Cody loved seeing his family on film. His number one fan, his mom, said, "Seeing Cody dance on stage, it's incredible. He was never, ever trained in this area and he's just amazing. I fly from Texas every week to see Cody perform. I love it when we have moments alone where I can ask him how he's really feeling, and pray that I give the right motherly advice to him. When Cody's dancing, he's going through it physically, but I am going through it emotionally. When it's tough on your children, it's tough on you. I'm so proud of Cody, I think he's become a deeper person; it's opened up a whole new world for him. I'll do everything I can to support him, but he's going to have to do it on his own." Cody loved the support, but the video didn't make his nerves go away—in fact, they probably made them worse!

Finally, host Tom Bergeron was ready to announce the contestants' standings and the audience's voting results. Cody felt his heart drop when Tom announced that Cody and Julianne, along with Warren Sapp and his partner, were in the bottom two, and that one of the couples would be leaving that night. Whichever couple remained at the end of the night would be dancing in the finals for the grand prize. There was an excruciating commercial break—Cody, Julianne, their families, and Cody's fans worldwide were on the edge of their seats. The break was only a few minutes long, but it felt like hours!

Finally, the show came back on and Tom was ready to announce the couple that would be moving on to the next round. Tom announced, "Cody and

Julianne, Warren and Kym, on this semi-final week of competition the couple with the lowest combined total and therefore leaving right now is . . ." there was an extended drum roll, and then Tom said after the pause, "Cody and Julianne." The camera cut over to Cody's mom, who looked sad and disappointed that her son was going home. Cody looked the same way as well—but he also looked really proud of all that he had accomplished. Cody and Julianne stood for a moment, soaking in the applause one final time, and then hugged each other and congratulated the remaining couple.

Cody and Julianne walked offstage with smiles on their faces to the sound of applause and screams of approval from the studio audience. Co-host Samantha Harris remarked to Cody, ". . . You always had lots of *Hannah Montana* fans, but your notoriety has grown so much from this time on this show. You have grown up so much . . . since starting this show. Hard to believe that you just graduated from high school not so long ago!"

At the end of the heartbreaking episode, a video

montage played of Cody and Julianne training and dancing together, and showed the two talking about what it was like to work together. Then the duo danced together one last time to the roar of the crowd as the lights in the studio dimmed. Cody may not have won *Dancing with the Stars* that season—that honor went to Brooke Burke and her partner (and Julianne's brother!) Derek Hough—but Cody did win legions of new fans along the way, and a lot of those fans were adults who were probably too old to have seen him on *Hannah Montana*! Plus, Cody had new, even bigger projects on the horizon. Appearing on *Dancing with the Stars* may have been a huge boost to his career, but it was time for the next big stage in the young phenom's life.

chapter nine

Ro and Co

What happens when you take two very talented teenage boys who love music, and add a computer, a webcam, and the Internet? If the two boys are best friends Cody Linley and Roshon Fegan, aka "Ya Boy Ro," you get *The Ro and Co Show*!

The two Disney stars became really good friends when they met during the 2008 Disney Channel Games. Roshon is a rapper who also goes by the name of 3inaRo, aka Young Ro, and he appeared in the Disney Channel original movie *Camp Rock*. In *Camp Rock*, Roshon played the role of Sander Loya, a rapper at the camp. In real life, Ro is a singer, actor, dancer, songwriter, producer, and rapper. The boys bonded immediately over their shared interests and hysterical sense of humor. One of the things the two had in common was their love of rapping. Cody's been known to bust a rap anytime, anywhere, even in the shower! He once told *Tigerbeat* magazine, "As I'm taking a shower I'll be rapping—I'll be half asleep rapping, and then by that time I'll figure out what I want to wear [for that day], it just goes from there." Cody and Ro wanted to share their love of music with their fans, so they decided that the best way to showcase their beatboxing, freestyling, and rapping skills was to create their own show and put it on the Internet. They decided to call it *The Ro and Co Show*—catchy!

On May 30, 2008, the two boys released their first show on YouTube. It was a funny sketch that showed the boys mock arguing back and forth about which one was the star of the show! They also told their fans, "Thank You so much for all the support and checking out 'The Ro and Co Show.' Check back soon for new videos! Be sure to subscribe to our channel and request us as a friend."

Their very first video was shot in Roshon's bedroom, so viewers really got an up close and personal glimpse of the boys. In the background, you can even see a really big SpongeBob SquarePants stuffed animal near the window, sneakers sitting on top of a dresser, and tons of posters tacked on the walls. Ro's room is just a typical teenage boy's bedroom, and fans loved that. For the first video, Roshon wore a red and black T-shirt, and Cody wore a red Montreal Canadiens hockey jersey. At the end of the video, Roshon and Cody told their fans that they would rap about any subject—all their viewers had to do was leave a comment with what they wanted the boys to rap about!

After that first episode, Cody and Roshon worked on a three-part episode filmed at the Key Club in Hollywood, California. The Key Club has live music every night and features up-and-coming acts (like Roshon and Cody!) alongside more established bands. Part one and two of the episode featured the boys rapping backstage with Verbal Ase, a beatboxer, and Jordan, a hype man, before going onstage for their first-ever live performance at the club. The performance was part three of their show, and Cody and Roshon did not disappoint. They were full of energy and spunk, and roamed all over the stage, jumping up and down, and shaking hands with audience members as they performed their song "Diss Me." Cody wore a red warm-up jacket over a white T-shirt and jeans. Roshon wore a printed T-shirt and baggy plaid, shorts. They both looked really cute, and had a ton of fun singing and meeting audience members.

Originally, Cody and Roshon promised to post a rap every single day on YouTube, but because they were busy with acting and auditioning, they just couldn't do it. But they didn't want to disappoint their fans, so they got their next video out in June. It was a two-part shout-out featuring lots of different songs. Roshon and Cody both wore black baseball hats and played the piano as they sang a duet. Just in case their fans wondered about why Cody and Roshon chose a piano for this particular song, Cody said, "We like to switch up our style. Sometimes we beatbox, sometimes it's rapping over instrumentals." These boys are definitely talented! Then Cody and Roshon rapped shout-outs to all their fans that left them comments on YouTube. Cody got a request to rap about his home state, Texas, and Ro was asked to rap about Los Angeles, his hometown. Other topics they rapped about were hair, guitars, iPod cases, batteries, Adidas and Supra kicks, and dental floss! Fans loved the personal touch to these videos, and kept coming back for more. Everybody hoped to see their shout-out featured next on *The Ro and Co Show.*

Ro and Co's next episode was called "Labor Day Chillin." It included a lot of fun moments, like Cody and Roshon rapping in Ro's bedroom and in the studio, and Cody's car breaking down! Another episode called "Happy Holidays" combined two of the boys' favorite things: rapping and pranking people! Cody and Roshon brought a video camera into a store and busted out a rap right then and there. The fans thought it was hysterical, and Cody and Roshon had a great time filming it.

Cody and Roshon put out new episodes of *The Ro*

and Co Show as often as they can, though it's sometimes hard, because both boys have busy schedules. The effort is worth it, though. Roshon and Cody both love expressing themselves musically, and cherish the opportunity to interact with their fans directly through shout-outs. Cody was collecting fans all over the place! He was no longer just the cute boy who stole Miley Cyrus's heart on *Hannah Montana*. He was also the boy who could dance a mean tango, and then hit the studio and rap! It was official: Cody Linley could do it all!

chapter ten

More Cody to Come

Cody has always been a very active guy who loves competing and trying new things. He's bursting with energy and talent, which means that he's always looking for new and better projects to take on. Even when Cody isn't filming, he tours the country making appearances at hockey games, award shows, and other events. Cody joined the *Dancing with the Stars* tour on January 4, 2009, for a performance at the American Airlines Center in Dallas, Texas, where he danced the jitterbug with Edyta. Cody loved getting the chance to reunite with his fellow castmates, but doesn't have plans to continue the nationwide tour because of other commitments. So what was next for this hot, young star?

Right before his stint on *Dancing with the Stars*, Cody took on a role that was very close to his heart. As a devout Christian, Cody was proud to be included as a voice in *Word of Promise Next Generation—New Testament*. Word of Promise is a twenty-CD set that was produced by actor Jim Caviezel from *Passion of the Christ* and stars Corbin Bleu, Alyson Stoner, Emily Osment, and other young stars with Cody. Cody originally auditioned for the role of Matthew, but was later awarded the role of Jesus. Cody and his fellow cast members recorded voices for this audio version of the Bible for kids. It was a great experience for the young star. Cody told parenting.com, "The best part of this was being able to keep my relationship with God in my day job." Because of his time spent voicing Joe Hardy in the Hardy Boys video game, Cody was a natural on set. The CD set was released in mid-November, 2008, while Cody was busy dancing with Julianne on *Dancing with the Stars*.

After that, Cody worked on a thriller, the independent movie *Forget Me Not*, with co-stars Brie

Gabrielle from *Hannah Montana* and Carly Schroeder from *Lizzie McGuire*. *Forget Me Not* is an edgy, modern-day horror movie that takes place in a small town. Cody plays Eli Channing, the brother of Carly's character, Sandy Channing. Sandy and her friends accidentally wake up a vengeful ghost, and one by one, Sandy's friends start to disappear. It was a challenging but rewarding role for Cody. It was his first R-rated feature, and he played a supernatural bad guy. Cody had to wear a lot of makeup for the role, and told the *Fort Worth Star-Telegram*, " . . . I went through three hours of prosthetics and makeup, and they turned my face into a dead fiend, a crazy monster with skin peeling off." A release date for the movie has not been set, so keep an eye out for it in the future!

Cody also filmed a ton of television commercials after his stint on *DWTS*, including a commercial for the fast food restaurant Zaxby's with fellow Disney star Alyson Stoner. And of course you can still catch Cody as Jake Ryan, Miley Cyrus's love interest on *Hannah Montana*.

Cody's star is shining bright and looks to shine brighter and brighter in the future. As he told *Hollywood Exclusive*, "With all the projects that have come my way, it's definitely been an awesome year. I'm so thankful for everything that's happened." In a recent interview with *My Fox–LA*, Cody talked a little bit about what he planned to do next. He said, "I'm going to just keep working. I mean, I've been having a blast on *Dancing with the Stars*. It's been crazy. It's opened a lot of opportunity for me, so I'm excited to go wherever. I'm a young guy, I want to go everywhere, and do everything. I'm working on music, I sing, I rap, I play guitar, so I've been writing some songs and stuff, so eventually I'll do an album. But in the immediate future [I'll] definitely [do] films." Fans weren't surprised to hear that Cody plans to release an album sometime in the future. He has been studying with Texas vocal coach Linda Septien, who has worked with many famous singers, including fellow Texas native Jessica Simpson.

Cody had planned to make his singing debut at a

February 2008 hockey game in Grand Rapids, Michigan, but at the last moment, he changed his mind! He told *J-14* magazine that he backed out at the last minute because "performing up on stage is totally different than performing in front of a camera, it's almost like you've got your one shot." Always the perfectionist, Cody wants to make sure his vocals are in top form before anyone hears him singing on an album or live onstage. Rapping is something he does for fun. Belting out serious vocals is a lot more difficult. Be sure to look out for Cody's new album sometime in the future!

chapter eleven

Living the Dream

Cody waited until graduating from high school to make the move full-time to Los Angeles. When he did move into his condo, he brought a little bit of Texas with him: Cody's new roommates were also his best friends from home! Cody explained to *Tigerbeat* magazine, "I'm a very social person, growing up with a big family, I'm used to hanging out with my brothers and friends, so when I'm alone, I'm very bored." Plus, Cody's friends from Texas help to keep him grounded. Cody knows firsthand how difficult it is to live a normal life when almost everyone who sees you on the street recognizes you. He is definitely thankful for his fame, but wants his fans to know that he struggles with problems, just like any normal teenager. He told sidewalkstv.com, "No matter where you are in life; you're still going to have worries . . . the main thing you got to do is just find the happiness in what you're doing." And Cody definitely knows how to do that. Nothing makes him happier than hanging out with his Texan buds, his family, and good friends like Roshon Fegan. Cody told sidewalkstv.com, ". . . I try to keep . . . my family close to me no matter what and wherever I am, because they're really my core. They make me who I am as a person, not my career. You know?" When Cody isn't filming, he likes to spend his time playing the guitar, shooting hoops, going to the movies, washing his car, and just doing teenage boy stuff like goofing off with his friends. Cody loves Chik-fil-A, and has been known to drive over an hour to the only one that's near his house in California.

Being famous has a few big downsides, like everybody knows what's going on in your love life! Sometimes when Cody is out on a date, he gets followed by female fans who want to say hello—or scope out the competition! Cody told *J-14* magazine, "I took my girl to eat at the mall, and the second we walked out, these 10 girls ran up to us and were like, 'Oh my God!' They kept telling the girl she was so lucky. That's weird when you're on a date." Talk about an embarrassing moment! Cody really loves his fans, though, so he always makes sure to stop for pictures or a quick autograph session, even if he is on a date! He even told *J-14* magazine, "I love my fans, it's so cool being able to make someone's day just by taking a picture with them. I look at those times when I'm signing autographs as a cool way to meet new people." But if Cody really doesn't want to be recognized, he admits that he'll wear a disguise to the mall!

Another aspect of Cody's love life that all his fans knew about was his relationship with fellow Disney star Demi Lovato. Cody met Demi when she was only nine years old. The two were paired together to work on a scene when they were a little bit older, and the rest is history! Even though he was shy to talk about it, Cody told *J-14* magazine a few details of the relationship he had with Demi. He said, "She's younger than me, so I never looked at her any other way. But when we did that scene together, it wasn't a romantic scene, and once I really got to know her, I really liked her a lot. She's one of the few girls who can really make me laugh. She's confident. And she's an amazing actress and singer."

Cody liked Demi so much that he asked her out! On one particular date, Cody was so determined to impress the brunette cutie, he wore a tie for their dinner date at the Cheesecake Factory. But he sort of blew it when his car broke down and he was late to pick her up. Cody told seventeen.com, ". . . We went out to eat and I was explaining to her, 'Yeah, my car, I'm sorry, it broke down,' and as I'm saying that, it starts making a crazy noise again! And I was like, 'Oh, oh, oh no,' and she was like, 'What's happening?' I was like, 'Nothing, it's all good.' She's like, 'Are you sure?' So I had to stop the car and get out. Demi was really sweet. She held the light for me and put in her car repair advice . . . she's kind of a technology geek in a way. I was trying to use my iPhone to see the engine, and she took my phone away, went to settings, and made the light brighter so I could see better." Talk about a memorable beginning to a relationship!

The two stars dated for a while, but eventually their busy schedules got in the way of their budding romance. Demi was busy working on an album in Miami, spending time with her family in Puerto Rico, and working on her new television show, *Sonny with a Chance*. Plus, she was getting ready to go on tour with the Jonas Brothers to promote her album. Meanwhile, Cody was busy working on various television projects, like *Hannah Montana*. Even though the adorable couple texted, e-mailed, and talked on the phone, it wasn't enough. Demi and Cody mutually decided to take a break from their relationship in May, 2008. Demi told *M* magazine, "We'll always be best friends." Cody felt the same way, and told *M* magazine, "Demi is really close to me and is a great friend. We dated in the past, but were both too busy and it just didn't work out. The great thing is we went back to being friends right away."

Even though Cody really liked Demi, he doesn't usually like to date other stars, even if the tabloids like to make up rumors about Cody's off-screen romances with his *Hannah Montana* co-stars. Cody told *Tigerbeat* magazine that, "I like someone who is fun, not someone who is just trying to be pretty. I'm romantic so I'll bring a different kind of flower and she'll be happy." This is good news for girls everywhere! Cody's mom Cathy told *J-14*, "[Cody] doesn't tell me anything about girls, but he's really sweet to them." She then described Cody's ideal girlfriend as "someone who sees who he is and who's not spoiled. An independent girl who keeps him in check. Somebody who is understanding, forgiving and fun. He likes girls who keep him from being bored!" Cody is a cute guy with a great heart—and he knows how to treat his girlfriend like a princess! It doesn't get much better than that.

chapter twelve

Cha-cha with Cody

When Cody was growing up in Texas, his mom asked if he wanted to take dance lessons. According to *BOP* magazine, Cody replied, "I don't want to dance, give me a soccer ball." When Cody was a teen, he wouldn't even dance with his date at the school dance because he was nervous! But when *Dancing with the Stars* asked Cody to become a contestant, he said yes because he knew it was good to try new things, even though he was afraid. Soon enough, Cody's dance partner Julianne had turned his entire attitude around! In dancing, "I found something I really love," Cody told *BOP*. "It's all about having fun!" If Cody had never said yes, he never would have learned that dancing was one of his secret talents.

If you want to learn to dance, follow Cody's example! Don't be nervous, relax, and stay open-minded. Oh, and make sure to practice as often as you can! In an interview with *BOP* magazine, Cody gave great advice for all the aspiring dancers out there. His most important piece of advice? "It's all about letting loose and having fun."

CODY'S TIPS FOR LEARNING HOW TO DANCE ARE:

1. Have fun.
2. Stay focused.
3. Pay attention and listen to your partner.
4. Be open to trying new things.
5. Practice every day, for at least an hour.
6. Relax when dancing.
7. Listen to the music and follow the beats.
8. Eat a healthy diet so you have lots of energy and can dance longer.
9. Cross-train your muscles. Cody lifted weights for an hour every day when he was learning

how to dance with Julianne.

10. Laugh a lot. Cody credits Julianne's sense of humor for making it easier for him to learn and have a good time doing something he never tried before.

chapter thirteen

Fun, Fast Cody Facts

Do you think you're Cody Linley's biggest fan? Maybe you've DVRed every single one of Cody's *Hannah Montana* episodes. Or you subscribe to *The Ro and Co Show*, and have even asked for a shout-out. You watched every episode of *Dancing with the Stars* live, and own copies of *Hoot, Miss Congeniality, Cheaper by the Dozen,* and R.L. Stine's *The Haunting Hour: Don't Think About It*. Maybe you sang along with Cody when he posted his own awesome version of Oasis's hit song "Wonderwall" on his MySpace page. Maybe so— but listen up, Cody fans! These are important facts that every Cody fanatic should know by heart.

FULL NAME: Cody Martin Linley

DATE OF BIRTH: November 20, 1989

HOMETOWN: Lewisville, Texas

HEIGHT: 5'8"

HAIR COLOR: naturally brown

SIBLINGS: older brother Chad, step-brothers Jimmy, Ben, Scotty, and Jason

BIOLOGICAL PARENTS: Cathy Linley Sullivan and Lee Linley

STAR SIGN: scorpio

NICKNAME: Co or Code-man

HOBBIES: playing guitar, beatboxing, rapping, and hanging out with friends

FAVORITE INSTRUMENTS: electric and acoustic guitar

FAVORITE MUSICIANS: Common, Kanye West, Tenacious D, Jack Johnson, Jay-Z, and The Beatles

FAVORITE MUSIC: country, rap, and rock

FAVORITE TV SHOWS: *Entourage* and *Da Ali G Show*

FAVORITE DAY OF THE WEEK: Friday

FAVORITE SAYING: "Shoot for the stars."

FAVORITE WEBSITE: acneheroes.com—he's a spokesperson for the site

FAVORITE CLOTHING: cowboy boots

FAVORITE STORE: American Eagle

FAVORITE ACTORS: Kevin Bacon, Leonardo DiCaprio, Owen Wilson, and Tom Hanks

FAVORITE EMOTICONS: :| , : - { }

FAVORITE PIZZA: Hawaiian-style

FAVORITE FAST FOOD: Chik-fil-A

FAVORITE MEAL: steak and sweet potatoes

FAVORITE PIE: sweet potato pie with marshmallows

FAVORITE BREAKFAST CEREAL: Banana Nut Crunch, but Cocoa Krispies are a close second

FAVORITE DRINK: iced sweet tea

FAVORITE CANDY: Orbit gum and chocolate

FAVORITE COOKIE: Girl Scout Cookies—Samoas

FAVORITE COLOR: green

CELEBRITY CRUSH: Jessica Alba

MOST PRIZED POSSESSION: his iPhone

PETS: two terriers named Yogi and Ellie

FAVORITE SPORTS: basketball and ice hockey

FAVORITE ATHLETE: LeBron James

FAVORITE COLLEGE SPORTS TEAM: University of Texas's football team—the Texas Longhorns

FAVORITE FOOTBALL TEAM: Dallas Cowboys

FAVORITE MOVIES: *Oceans 11, Titanic, Catch Me If You Can, Road to Perdition,* and *Pirates of the Caribbean 1 & 2*

IF HE WASN'T AN ACTOR, HE'D LIKE TO BE: a basketball player

ODDS AND ENDS

- Likes to doodle smiley faces
- Is sometimes mistaken for Jason Dolley
- Elementary School: Degan Elementary School
- High School: Lewisville High School—home of the Fighting Farmers
- When living in Los Angeles during the school year, attended Options For Youth—an independent education program for actors
- Is the second-youngest celebrity competitor ever chosen for *Dancing with the Stars* (17-year-old

Olympic gymnast Shawn Johnson is the youngest)

- Once auditioned for Harry Potter
- Addicted to toothpicks
- First appeared in a Disney show in 2004—as Daryl on *That's So Raven*
- Car: '98 Mustang convertible
- Has appeared in commercials for JC Penney and McDonalds
- Has always wanted to be a contestant on *Family Feud*
- Doesn't understand the popularity of girls wearing Crocs
- Dream job: playing James Bond
- Favorite feature on a girl: her smile
- First thing he notices in a guy/girl: sense of humor
- One year dressed as basketball player Dennis Rodman for Halloween
- Most ticklish spot: feet

Cody's a really loyal guy. He's still friends with the kids from his elementary school. Wherever Cody has worked, he's always made lasting friendships with guys and gals. But Cody is also a kind of private person and counts his family, especially his mom and his brothers, as his closest friends. Could you be one of Cody's friends? Cody has friends he likes to hang out and play sports with—he also has rapping and acting buds. Which type of Cody bud are you?

1) IT'S A GORGEOUS, SUNNY LOS ANGELES DAY. YOU HAVE THE ENTIRE DAY TO DO WHATEVER YOU WANT. YOU:

A. go outside and shoot some hoops.

B. go to the movies and see the latest flick.

C. find a Chik-fil-A or order in a pizza, and play video games.

2) YOU AND CODY ARE ACTING TOGETHER IN A MOVIE. IT'S A RAINY DAY, SO THE SCENES YOU WERE SUPPOSED TO SHOOT OUTSIDE ARE POSTPONED. YOU AND CODY DECIDE TO:

A. play ping-pong.

B. go somewhere quiet to study the script and run lines.

C. grab your guitars and jam.

3) YOU, CODY, AND SOME OF YOUR FRIENDS ARE HANGING OUT AT THE MALL. YOU'VE WANDERED IN AND OUT OF ALL THE STORES, AND NOW YOU'RE BORED. DO YOU:

A. start pranking each other?

B. hit the food court and chat with fans?

C: go to the music store and check out the instruments?

4) YOU'RE IN A RUT AND ARE THINKING OF FINDING SOMETHING NEW TO LEARN. YOU:

A. decide it's better to practice the skills that you have to make them better.

B. attempt a hobby that you've never done before, just to see if you can.

C. decide to work on your hidden talent—who knows where that will lead?

IF YOU GOT . . .

MOSTLY As—You're one of Cody's sporty friends. You hate to waste time indoors when you could be outdoors throwing a football, just like he and Emily Osment did on the set of *The Haunting Hour*. You like to be busy all the time, just like Cody!

MOSTLY Bs—You're one of Cody's acting friends. Honing the craft is as important to you as it is to Cody. You both want to give 100 percent to any project you're in. You and Cody like to work hard and see your efforts pay off!

MOSTLY Cs—You're one of Cody's down-home friends. You and Cody like to take time to meet new people and just chill. You and Cody are both laid-back, but still want to be the best that you can be at whatever you put your mind to. You might even practice the guitar on the down-low, only to surprise people when you give a recital!

chapter fourteen

Cody Online

You might think you know everything there is to know about Cody, but he's always giving new interviews, signing up for new projects, and working on new raps. There's always something new going on in Cody's life, and the best place to get all the latest news is online. There are tons of Cody websites on the Internet. Just make sure to get a parent's permission before going online. Also, never talk to someone you don't know online—Cody would want you to be careful when you're on the Internet! Don't worry if one of the sites listed below is no longer around. Websites come and go, but with a little searching, you can always find all the Cody information that you need. Who knows—

maybe you can start your own Cody fansite someday with all the information from this book!

HTTP://WWW.MYSPACE.COM/THEOFFICIALCODYLINLEY

This is Cody's official MySpace page. It features all the latest Cody Linley news and is updated fairly often.

HTTP://WWW.MYSPACE.COM/CODYLINLEYMUSIC

This is Cody's secondary MySpace page, dedicated entirely to his budding music career! Check here for info about Cody's forthcoming album, and to listen to some of his raps!

WWW.CODYMLINLEY.COM

This is Cody's official fansite, and the place to go to read his blog, look at photos of Cody, and visit his store. If you want to buy anything from Cody's store, get permission from your parents first.

HTTP://WWW.YOUTUBE.COM/USER/THEROANDCOSHOW

This is Cody and Roshon's YouTube site for their show, *The Ro and Co Show*. You can find every episode of *Ro and Co* here. It's also the place to go to subscribe to the show and leave messages for the boys.

HTTP://WWW.YOUTUBE.COM/DCGAMES2008

This is where to go to watch Cody interviewing Disney stars on the red carpet at the 2008 Disney Channel Games.

WWW.LINLEYLOVE.ORG

A fansite devoted to all things Cody Linley, this website has scans from every magazine that Cody has appeared in, as well as video interviews, photographs, and more.

HTTP://CODYLINLEY.FANGAP.COM

This is another Cody fansite—with lots of news and pictures.

WANT TO SEND CODY A CARD OR LETTER?
YOU CAN WRITE CODY AT:

Cody Linley

c/o *Hannah Montana*

Disney Channel

3800 W. Almeda Ave

Burbank, CA 91505